THE SISTER SPLIT

THE SISTER SPLIT

AURIANE DESOMBRE

DELACORTE PRESS

Text copyright © 2023 by Auriane Desombre
Jacket art copyright © 2023 by Celia Krampien

All rights reserved. Published in the United States by Delacorte Press,
an imprint of Random House Children's Books,
a division of Penguin Random House LLC, New York.

Delacorte Press is a registered trademark and the colophon is a trademark
of Penguin Random House LLC.

Visit us on the Web! rhcbooks.com

Educators and librarians, for a variety of teaching tools,
visit us at RHTeachersLibrarians.com

Library of Congress Cataloging-in-Publication Data is available upon request.
ISBN 978-0-593-56868-2 (trade) — ISBN 978-0-593-56869-9 (lib. bdg.) —
ISBN 978-0-593-56870-5 (ebook)

The text of this book is set in 12-point Palatino LT.
Interior design by Ken Crossland

Printed in the United States of America
1st Printing
First Edition

FOR THOMAS

AND FOR CAROLINE

AND FOR OUR INTERWOVEN,

INTERLACED CHILDHOODS

CHAPTER
ONE

Ice cream always tastes better when it's banned. Well, not *banned*, exactly, but Mom specifically told me to come straight home after school today because she has some kind of special announcement. Friday is mint chocolate chip day, though. It says so in curly green ink at the top of Saskia's planner, in the space where she's supposed to write her homework for language arts. We've been using it to plan our hunt for the best ice cream shop in the neighborhood instead. And I'm not about to skip mint chocolate chip day.

No matter how curious I am about Mom's announcement.

"Okay, let's get down to business," Saskia says, clicking her pen.

I nod through bites of ice cream, pulling my map out of my backpack and laying it carefully on the table between us. I spent all of math class drawing it. Mom's worried about my math grade, but perfecting my map-making abilities is way more fun than probability. No matter how important Ms. Albright insists percentages and negative numbers are, I already know that the probability of using them in real life is less than zero. Maps, though, I need in real life all the time. Right now, for example, a map is all I need for us to get the perfect summer plan down.

Saskia leans over, holding her melty ice cream off to the side so it doesn't dribble onto my outline of downtown Manhattan. I only drew the parts of the city where we're allowed to go on our own. Our moms agreed that we're both allowed to travel within a fifteen-block radius of our apartments.

Popping the crunchy tip of the cone into my mouth, I dig through my backpack for the stickers I picked out from a stationery store last month. They cost more than the ones I found at Duane Reade, but they include a bunch of pizza slices with googly eyes, and that was worth the extra $1.25. I peel one off and stick it over Carmine Street on the map.

"We have to start with Joe's Pizza, obviously."

The end of sixth grade is in just one week, which means we have a week to plan a whole summer's worth of outings. There are endless summer days to fill, with just the two of us.

First up: a pizza tour.

I dot my map with pizza stickers while Saskia draws ice cream cones over our favorite shops. She gets the curl of the scoop right every time.

"Okay, what's next?" she asks. "Cupcake wars challenge? Museum art reenactment? Fancy tea shop party? Beach day?"

"Beach day," I say with a wistful sigh. Getting caught in ocean waves is the best kind of fun. The beach kind of sucks in the city, though. Coney Island is great and all, but it's always packed with people, and Mom has to assign family swimming shifts so that there's someone to sit on the towel and watch our stuff.

Instead, I type *tea places* into the maps app on the cell phone Mom finally let me get a few months ago. I'm just about to copy the first place I find onto our map when the phone rings.

"Autumn?" Mom says as soon as I pick up.

"We're on our way home," I say quickly.

Mom laughs. "I know you stopped for ice cream."

I groan. The only downside of having a phone is

3

the Find My app, which Mom insists on using to make sure I don't get kidnapped. Or stop for ice cream.

"It's mint chip day," I say.

"As much as I hate to interrupt mint chip day," Mom says, and I can hear the smile in her voice, "it's family game night. I need you home, okay?"

I guess that's one other downside to finally having a phone: Mom can always call to force me to leave Saskia and go hang out with Harrison, aka Harristinks.

Every Friday used to be family game night. We'd order pizza and play Monopoly. My big brother, George, would always let me have the lucky race car but be a real sore loser about it when I bought his favorite hotels. Mom would then sneak up for the win as we argued. The winner—always, always Mom— would get to pick our movie for the night, and she'd make us watch something that sounded super dumb but would turn out to be great.

But two years ago Mom started dating Harrison, and I got to kiss family game night goodbye. It became family game night plus Harrison and his boring daughter, Linnea, who always ends up ruining it. Harristinks is a science teacher, and having him over for game night feels exactly like inviting Ms. Albright to my living room to teach me more about negative numbers. Last time, he spent the whole night telling us about some lesson he was planning to teach on the phases of the moon and the shifting constellations, which made even Monopoly boring. On the rare occasions he's not talking about space—and seriously, they're *rare*—he's joining forces with Mom to try and make me bond with Linnea.

Harrison doesn't even live in New York; he lives in some random town in Connecticut, which means they have to take a long train ride to come ruin our Friday tradition. That's how determined he is. I don't get why Mom invites him. Soggy cardboard is funnier than his jokes.

Ever since he started coming around, I've done my best to skip family game night, but Mom always sees right through my attempts.

"But, Mom—"

"Start heading home right now, Autumn," she says sternly. "I have a special announcement today, and I don't want you to be late."

I sit up straighter, curiosity spiking through me again. "What is it?"

Maybe she broke up with Harristinks. She could do so much better than a boyfriend so boring he needed to go all the way to space to try and find a personality.

5

"I'll tell you when you get here," Mom says. "Hurry."

She says goodbye and hangs up.

"I have to head home," I say as I carefully fold the map, and Saskia's shoulders slump. "Mom says she has a special announcement."

Saskia and I leave the ice cream store and cross the street to the subway entrance. Outside, it smells like city summer: hot garbage and chocolate ice cream. The air gets hotter and stuffier as we go down the stairs to the subway platform.

Saskia crosses her fingers at me. "Maybe the announcement is that your mom broke up with Harristinks."

I laugh. Saskia and I are always on the same wavelength, like our thoughts are written in our eyes in a language only the two of us can read. "That's what I'm hoping."

I hate Harrison, and not just because he's the most boring person I've ever met in my entire life. Boyfriends aren't supposed to be a thing for moms. Before Harrison came along, Mom spent all her free time with George and me. Family game night was just the three of us, making the rules exactly the way we like them to be. Saturdays were for cool art projects and exploring our neighborhood. And every evening after school, we'd have dinner as a family, and George would teach me and Mom new recipes he found after scouring his collection of cookbooks. Now most of the weekend is Mom posting the emergency phone numbers on the fridge before she waltzes out the door to go on a *date*, leaving George to watch me.

Boyfriends are supposed to be for my friends, who keep asking each other *who do you like?* during Truth or Dare at sleepovers and carefully track who's asking out who. I always pretend to have a crush on Tim Walton even though I don't really care about him that much. It just feels easier to pretend I like a boy than try to explain why I still haven't had a crush on anyone at all.

Just because Mom and Dad got divorced and he went away to California when he got remarried to Can-I-Talk-To-The-Manager Lisa about two seconds after my first birthday doesn't suddenly turn *boyfriend* into a Mom-appropriate word. Because when it comes to Mom, *boyfriend* is just a synonym for *ditch Autumn with George as a babysitter and go roam around the city with the world's most boring space nerd instead of hanging out with my supercool daughter.*

Saskia taps my shoulder. "You okay?"

The train pulls into the station, brakes screeching, and I wait until it comes to a stop before answering. "Yeah. I just hate Harristinks."

"That's why we named him Harristinks," she says with a grin as we get onto the subway car. "Well, that and his cologne."

I grin at the memory of the day I told Saskia about meeting Harristinks. He'd smelled thick with body spray, the kind that always clogs the halls at school when we pass a group of eighth-grade boys. I haven't smelled it on him since, but he stinks enough metaphorically that the nickname stuck.

"Maybe after today you'll never see him again," Saskia says.

That gets me to smile. "You're right."

Saskia gets off just two stops after we get on. I wave goodbye when she stands up, pulling the corners of my lips down. She mirrors me, making a sad face as she leaves the train.

I ride one more stop by myself, knocking my knees together as I wait. As soon as the train hurtles into my station, I jump out of my seat, bubbling with eagerness to get home. Maybe the announcement really will be good news.

I run up the sidewalk until I make it to our building. I take the stairs to our seventh-floor walk-up three at a time, my muscles stretching under me. It's way too many steps to take at once. I trip over the last one and end up sprawled all over the landing at the top of the staircase.

My brother swings our apartment door open, his eyebrows raised so high they disappear behind his scraggly bangs.

"You okay down there?" he asks.

I purse my lips at him as I get up. George had a growth spurt last summer, and now he thinks he's all that just because he's almost six feet tall and almost done with high school. If you ask me, that's a lot of *almost*s, but he thinks it gives him bragging rights.

"I'm fine, Cocoa Puffs."

We always call each other cereal names. I threw a temper tantrum when I was a kid once (well, more than once, I did a few of those when I was a toddler, but one time in particular) because I thought it was stupid that my name didn't change with the seasons. George, who was ten at the time, calmed me down when he called me Cheerios after the cereal box Mom had on the kitchen table. The temper tantrums went away, but our habit of calling each other by cereal names stuck. Cocoa Puffs is our insult cereal, because both of us think it tastes like sugar barfed into a plastic bag.

"Autumn?" Mom's voice comes from inside, and I forget about being fake mad at George.

I bounce past him and shrug my backpack off by the coat hooks. It lands on the floor with a thud. I kick off my shoes next to it and run into the living room to dive onto our couch.

"Are we going to start with Monopoly or Settlers of Catan?" I ask, propping my feet up on the coffee table.

Mom comes in, her palms hugging a mug of coffee. She nudges my feet off the table with her toes, and I tuck them under one of the couch pillows.

"It's been ages since we've played Catan," she says. "But let's wait until Harrison and Linnea get here."

Her words make my stomach go queasy. The news can't be *that* good if Harrison and Linnea are still coming.

"Should we prep our dinner order for later?" George asks. He's always thinking about our next meal. The Chinese take-out menu dangles from his fingers, even though it's useless because we always order the same exact thing from this place: chicken and broccoli, beef lo mein, pork fried dumplings, two types of fried rice, a large order of soup, sesame chicken, and spring rolls. The first time we ordered, they sent our food with seven forks, and we were too embarrassed to tell them it was just the three of us.

"Let's skip to the announcement. I had—" I cough.

Mom didn't technically give me permission for the ice cream. "I'm not that hungry."

"I know you had ice cream, so you don't have to pretend. Besides, we're waiting for Harrison and Linnea to get here," Mom says in that reasonable adult tone she uses when I am being especially not-reasonable and not-adult.

George sighs. "Since you're all content to let me starve, I'm setting up Settlers of Catan."

I sit up to help him spread the pieces out on the table. We're arguing over how to arrange the land tiles for the game when the key spins in the lock. I jump at the noise. It's been months since Mom gave Harrison a key to our apartment, but the sound of someone else letting themselves in when all three of us are home still gives me the creeps.

The door opens and Harristinks himself walks in, Linnea trailing behind him. She gives me a small wave, which I return. Mom always says we should be friends, the way grown-ups do when they assume that just because kids are the same age, they automatically have to be best buddies. It doesn't make any sense. It's not like Mom is best friends with every random forty-four-year-old she meets, so I don't see why I should be friends with every twelve-year-old she finds.

Mom bounces up from her chair and crosses the room to kiss Harrison. I look away, because *blech*, and George makes a face at me. Harristinks holds Mom's hand as they sit next to me on the couch. Linnea sits cross-legged on the floor by the table, staring at the game.

Mom gives me a pointed look. I sigh at her before shifting to face Linnea.

"How was your week?" I ask.

She mumbles a response so quietly, I can't make out her words at all. Her voice is always so meek and small and painfully shy that it's impossible to hear her. It doesn't matter, though. We've had the same polite exchange so many times that I know exactly what she's said without needing to hear the words.

"That's great," I say back. "Mine was good too."

She says something else, and I lean forward, straining to make out the words.

"Sorry?" I ask.

Red stains splotch across her pale cheeks as she forces herself to speak up. "I was just saying I've never played this game before."

"It's super competitive," I tell her. I mean it as a reassurance, because competitive games are the *best*, but it makes her eyes go wide with fright. I quickly look away to stop myself from rolling my eyes. I swear, this girl is so timid, it's a miracle she doesn't have a nervous breakdown every time she spots her own shadow.

"Before we get started, I think it's time for an announcement," Mom says. She and Harristinks are still holding hands, and the sight makes my stomach flip-flop like it's just been thrown in the washer. If they're clutching each other like that, the announcement isn't gonna be that they broke up.

"Harrison and I have been talking," Mom goes on, exchanging a look and a little smile with Harristinks. Last time Harrison and Mom did some talking, he got invited to every single game night and ruined my favorite family tradition. What is it going to be this time?

Mom smiles wider as Harrison looks down at me.

"We're engaged," he says.

Mom lifts her left hand, where she's slipped on a sparkly diamond ring that she must've kept hidden in her pocket until now.

George immediately gets up to hug them. "Congratulations," he says, like a traitorous traitor.

Linnea gasps, and I can't tell if she's happy or if her insides feel as burnt to ash as mine do.

I stare at the ring. "What?"

"We're getting married, honey," Mom says.

"I know what *engaged* means," I say. My question

is, what would make you do something like that? But I don't dare actually ask again in front of Harristinks.

Mom and Harrison glance at each other before she turns back to me. "Well, we've been dating for two years, and we love each other very much, and we want to be a family. So we're getting married."

We want to be a family? What are George and I, rotten potatoes? Is Mom forgetting that she already *has* a perfectly good family? It takes all my effort not to wrinkle my nose. "So Harrison is going to come live here?"

George is going off to college at the end of the summer, so I guess Linnea can have his room. But then where will George stay when he comes to visit? I made him promise to visit *lots*.

"Actually, that's the second part of the announcement," Mom says. She reaches over with the hand that's not clutching Harrison's and squeezes my fingers. "We're going to move into Harrison's house in East Hammond this summer."

All my thoughts screech like the subway braking at the station, my mind going blank. I'm so shocked I can't even take a breath in.

What?

We're going to *what*?

"Us?" I ask. "Go to them?"

My thoughts come back in quick snippets, as if I'm

flipping through a photo album too fast: My bedroom. The desk with all the art supplies I use for my maps. School, the classroom where I'm supposed to start seventh grade next fall. My favorite table at my favorite ice cream spot.

Saskia.

Our summer plans.

All our adventures.

All of them . . . gone.

Out of everything I stand to lose, not seeing Saskia every day hurts the worst. Worse than the time I fell off my scooter and had to get four stitches after I gashed my knee open. Worse than the time I forgot my lines for my scene in the fifth-grade musical and even the other kids onstage laughed at me. Worse than when Dad moved to California without me. At least he didn't drag me away from my home and everyone I love to live in East Hammond.

I can't lose my best friend in the world. I can't miss all our summer plans, and all the ones we would've had next year and the year after that. I splurged on the pricey stickers.

"Yes," Mom says. She's smiling huge in a way that makes everything hurt worse. It's like she doesn't see the way I'm scrunching my nose so I don't cry in front of Linnea. Or maybe she does, and she just doesn't care. "We're going to go as soon as school ends next week. I think we can use the time to get settled into our new home before the wedding."

My skin feels hot, like sparks are flying off me every time I move.

"Well, I don't think so," I say, gasping for air. "I have plans for the summer, big plans. Saskia and I were going to—"

"Yeah, and it's my last summer before college. I was—" George starts, but Mom cuts us off.

"You have time to say goodbye to your friends before we go." Mom looks at both of us. I can feel Linnea's eyes boring into me, too, and I shrivel as Mom keeps glaring at me. "This is family. It's important."

I stare at her, my lower lip trembling. Saskia and I were finally going to be allowed to roam the city by ourselves. I was going to force her to join our summer camp art show, because her paintings are so good that they need to be shown off, even though she's too scared to display them. She was going to teach me how to draw cute little icons to make my maps prettier.

It was finally our chance to spend a whole summer together, away from adults, making plans and exploring on our own terms. Just the two of us.

And now, thanks to Mom, all of it is ruined.

Anger spikes through me, roping its way through

my body like it's a physical thing. I can feel it curling around in my chest, like smoke hardening into something more solid. I get up and run out of the living room. Mom calls after me, but George's voice overlaps with hers until the two of them are caught in their own argument. And I'm left all alone.

CHAPTER
TWO

I stare at the empty cardboard box propped open on the kitchen counter in front of me. I've never packed a cardboard box in my life. I have no idea what to put in first.

Mom breezes in from her studio, where she spends her workdays illustrating picture books. Even though it's early, her fingers are already smudged with ink.

"What's going on?" she asks with a smile.

"I just can't believe I have to move away from Saskia," I say glumly.

"Oh, honey, you can still keep in touch with your friend," she says as she opens a cabinet. "Want some cereal for breakfast?"

"Well, can we at least visit?" I ask, ignoring her question. My stomach is way too tight for cereal.

Mom ruffles my hair. "I know it's a big change, Autumn, but you'll make new friends. Keep in touch with Saskia, of course, but the point of this is to settle in as a new family. We're going to focus on spending time with Harrison and Linnea this summer and make a real home in East Hammond. Soon you won't even want to come back here." She waves the cereal box at me, raising an eyebrow.

I shake my head. I can't just shift from moving to East Hammond to eating breakfast as if the thought of ripping myself away from my best friend doesn't make me want to puke. There's no way I'll never want to come back to New York. This is right where I belong. Here, in our family apartment. The fact that Mom could even think that just proves that she's not listening to a word I say.

"We had important things planned," I remind her.

"You can make new plans in East Hammond," Mom says, her expression unmoved.

"That's not the same," I say. "Some of them are educational, you know," I add hopefully. "We want to go to a bunch of museums."

Mom sighs. "You'll get to explore East Hammond with Linnea all summer."

I grit my teeth. The thought of spending the whole summer struggling to hear Linnea's voice buried under her thick layers of shy awkwardness makes me want to scream. Mom doesn't get it. Maybe if she spent more time at home instead of with her stupid boyfriend, she would understand.

But then she opens her mouth and, as if to prove how much she doesn't know or care about me at all, says, "You'll get to learn how to ride a bike."

A bike. She's trading my best friend for a bike and smiling like it isn't the worst thing she's ever done to me.

"Where's George?" I ask. Arguing more is clearly pointless. It's not like she's going to hear me.

"He's packing his room," Mom says, pushing my box toward me. "Which is what you should be doing."

I huff, picking up the box and dragging it down the hall. Instead of going straight to my room, I kick open the door to George's room instead.

"How are you packing your boxes?" I ask, peering into the one open on his bed. His bookshelves are already bare, his closet's half empty, and he has four whole boxes taped closed and lined up by the wall.

"Slowly," he says with a sigh. "I wasn't expecting to have to do this all at once."

"This is slow?" I stare at his neat row of finished boxes.

"Why, how many have you done?" George asks.

I look down at the empty box in my hand, and he laughs.

"Why don't you call Saskia and ask her to help you?" he says. "It'll give you an excuse to hang out with her. And you clearly need some assistance."

"I—" I clear my throat. "I haven't exactly told her we're moving yet."

George reaches over and smacks my shoulder.

"*Ow,*" I shriek, even though it didn't hurt. Complaining about him is just one of my little-sister privileges.

"You're going to have to tell her eventually," George says, crossing his arms.

"Not if I convince Mom to let us stay," I say, copying his pose.

He reaches over and snatches my phone out of my pocket before I can stop him.

"Hey!" I reach for it, but he presses a few buttons on the screen and holds it up to my ear. It rings until I hear Saskia's voice.

"Hello?"

I gasp, reaching over to hit George.

"Autumn?"

"Hi," I say quietly as I walk out of George's room, leaving the box behind. I need some privacy for this conversation. "I . . . have some news."

21

"Did your mom break up with Harristinks?" Saskia asks. She sounds so eager, it makes me want to stop talking right now, hang up the phone, and hide under my bed so Mom doesn't notice she's left me behind when she leaves.

"Not exactly." I close the door to my bedroom and tuck myself back into bed, the blankets tight around my legs. It's not as comforting as I'd hoped it would be.

"What was the big announcement?"

"She . . ." I have no idea how to say the rest of the sentence. It's too horrible. I take a deep breath, letting all the words come out at once. "She and Harrison are getting married, and we all have to move to his stupid house in stupider East Hammond."

Saskia is quiet for a long time. I clutch the phone, my heart pounding in my fingertips as she processes the horrors I've just dumped on her.

"What?" she screeches.

"I know," I say. "It's awful. She's completely ruining my life."

"We can't let her," Saskia says, and then all I can hear is a beep followed by silence, because she's hung up.

● ● ●

I tried calling Saskia back, but she didn't answer. I have no idea where she's gone, but ten minutes later, Mom came to yell at me about how we have to finish packing by the end of the week and I need to stop procrastinating. So now I'm stuck in my room, just me and the still-empty cardboard box.

I scan my bookshelf on the other side of the room. I'll start by packing up the books. Then I can spend the whole summer hiding away from Harrison and a forced friendship with same-age Linnea, and Mom can't even be mad because she's always saying how great reading is for me.

The doorbell rings, chiming through the apartment. I ignore it until I hear Saskia's voice as Mom opens the front door.

I'm out of my bedroom in a flash.

"What are you doing here?" I ask, skidding down the hall to the front door. Mom steps out of my way right before I crash into her.

"I just wanted . . ." She glances up at Mom, her cheeks growing pink. "I just wanted to see you."

The sad look in her eyes makes a lump form in my throat. I don't know how to say goodbye to her.

I turn to Mom, leaning against the door as it swings on its hinge. "Is it okay if we go hang out for a bit?"

"I thought we could do some of our summer plans now?" Saskia adds. "Since we won't get to spend the summer together."

I turn to Mom, my eyes huge. She laughs at my expression.

"What a nice idea, girls," she says. "I suppose you can continue packing tonight. Turn Find My on, please, and send me a text every hour so that I know you're safe, and stay in the radius we agreed on, and be back by dinnertime, and—"

"Mom, it'll be fine," I say. "We're just going to go to a park or something, not go for a swim in the Hudson."

She chuckles, running a hand through my hair. "I just can't believe you're big enough to be out and about in the city by yourself."

"Just in time for us to leave," I point out, and the smile falls off Mom's face.

I slide my feet into my sneakers, grab my bag with my wallet and phone, and take Saskia's hand as we run down our hall to the staircase.

"Be safe," Mom calls after us. I wave to her before running down the stairwell so fast we almost trip over the last few steps. We race down another flight of stairs and barrel onto the sidewalk. Outside, the air is sticky with almost-summertime afternoon heat.

"So, where do you want to go?" I ask. My stomach grumbles as soon as I finish, and Saskia laughs.

"Wanna get food?" she asks.

I beam. "Always."

She grabs my hand, pulling me down the sidewalk. "I have an idea."

I perk up as I fall into step beside her, our hands swinging between us. The promise of food always gets me going. "Where?"

"It's a surprise," she says with a smile.

I keep asking questions as we get to the subway station, but Saskia cheerfully ignores me. The train is just pulling up when we get down to the platform, so I spend minimal time sweating my brains out before we pack ourselves into the crowded but cool subway car.

Every time I ask a question, Saskia swats me away with a playful smile, finally leading me off the subway three stops later. I gasp when she leads me down the sidewalk to Joe's Pizza. We get in the lunch-rush line, which spills over past the front doors of the restaurant onto the sidewalk.

I do a little hop when we get in line. "An excellent choice."

"Oh, this isn't the only place we're going," she says, smiling again.

I lean in. "Are you saying what I think you're saying?"

"Pizza tour," Saskia says, throwing her hands up toward Joe's sign.

I give a cheer, shimmying in place as I do my best rendition of a viral dance we taught ourselves at recess last week. Pizza tour has topped our list of summer adventures since we started planning for our vacation. I crane my neck, standing as high on my tiptoes as I can without toppling over. The line stretches too far out. I lower my heels back to the sidewalk, and my stomach growls.

Saskia laughs, poking me in the side, and I swat her hand, laughing.

"I was too busy moping to have lunch."

She tsks at me. "You're such a drama queen."

I purse my lips at her, even though it's true and we both know it. The line inches forward, and we shuffle up with it.

"I'm really going to miss you," she says, so quietly her voice is almost drowned out by the long honk of a passing cab.

I look at her, the lump in my throat returning. "I'm gonna miss you too."

"Promise to stay friends forever?" Saskia asks.

I stick out my pinky. "Duh. Always. No matter what."

She wraps her pinky around mine, and we shake our hands. There's no oath more solemn than a pinky swear, and even though nothing's changed, it makes me feel a tiny bit better to have the reassurance that Saskia is as determined as I am to keep our friendship just the same.

We get to the front of the line, and I slide my wad of bills across the counter in exchange for the perfect slice of pizza.

As soon as they hand me my paper plate, already a bit soggy from grease, I balance the pizza slice over my face and lower it into my mouth. The cheese immediately burns my tongue, but it's worth it.

"You've never looked more graceful," Saskia says. She's holding her paper plate primly, waiting for the slice to cool.

I purse my grease-stained lips at her. "Sorry I don't have your ridiculous willpower."

"You should be," she says.

As soon as we finish our slices (me in ten seconds and Saskia in eight thousand years), Saskia takes me to Prince Street Pizza, which has my favorite pepperoni slice in the city. By the time we make it to Artichoke Basille's Pizza, I can't even finish the enormous wad of bread and cheese they slide across the counter to me. My stomach feels like it's about to explode.

Which might not be such a bad thing. I bet if I exploded, Mom wouldn't make me go to East Hammond.

I dab at my lips with a paper napkin, but the grease lingers. It feels like a permanent part of who I am now.

"I don't think I can do any more pizza," I say.

Saskia pats her stomach. "I don't think I could do the last slice of pizza I just ate, to be honest."

I laugh. Artichoke pizza is good, but it's also the hugest slice I've ever seen in my life.

"What's next, then?" I say.

"Well, it was going to be dessert," Saskia says, "but I think we can skip that and go straight to the park."

After all the carbs I just shoveled into my mouth, I could use a few hours of lying in a sunny patch of grass with her.

We go to Washington Square Park, which is one of our favorite spots by school. It's typically full of college students on sunny weekends, but their school ends in May—*lucky*—so they've all gone home. The park is still busy, with families spread out on the lawn, street performers playing music or writing poems-on-demand on clacky typewriters, and little kids blowing bubbles into the fountain or waddling all over the park's teeny playground.

I reach up and pop a wayward bubble floating above my head as we find a sunny spot across from the fenced-in dog park and plop down. I lie back, the grass cool and dry against my skin, and stare up at the sky. The tall buildings block out the skyline in most of the city, which is part of why I love the park so much. If you just stare straight up, and block out your peripheral vision, it's blue all the way across.

Mom's favorite bit of unsolicited advice is to enjoy each moment, but all I can think about as I'm enjoying this moment is how much I'm going to miss it. More importantly, how much I'm going to miss *Saskia*. We're the best best friends in our grade. We do everything together. We have sleepovers whenever our parents let us, which is pretty much every week because we bug them about it so much. We have adventures and inside jokes and we know everything there is to know about each other. Favorite ice cream flavors, weirdest dreams we've ever had, all the little secrets that are too scary to tell my mom.

At least we promised to be friends forever. But even if we're promising forever, I still have to move. Forever is still not enough if it's apart.

"I think I know why I can't say goodbye to the city," I blurt out. "I'm not *supposed* to."

"What do you mean?" she asks.

"I'll find a way to come back," I tell her. "I can't leave here forever."

She looks sideways at me, and there's a flicker of hope in her starry eyes. "How?"

"I have no idea," I say, but I want the hope in her eyes to grow, so I bite my lip as I think. "I could run away."

"You'd just have to go back," Saskia points out. "The only way you could come back for good is if your mom decides not to marry Harristinks after all."

I slump back. "You're right."

I stare up at the sky, trying to think of a different plan. There has to be some way to get me back home. There just has to be. I can't say goodbye to this city and all the people in it. It's where I belong. If I had to draw out all the most important times of my life, they would fit onto a map of Manhattan. How am I supposed to leave it behind?

Saskia's right, I realize. The only way I get to come back to New York at the end of the summer is if Mom and Harrison don't get married.

Mom and Harrison *shouldn't* get married anyway. Mom illustrates picture books and always comes up with the best projects for us to do together. She wins at Monopoly every time and makes such funny jokes that even watching the most boring movie in the world becomes hilarious if I watch it with her. Even when she's being a total mom and trying to give me stupid advice, I can't help but love the time I spend with her. I've never even heard Harrison *try* to crack a good joke. All he ever wants to talk about is his totally blah job and practice his astronomy class lectures on us at the dinner table. My quirky, artistic, effortlessly cool mom can do so much better than plain dull Harristinks.

So that has to be the plan.

"If I want to come home," I say, "Mom and Harrison have to decide not to get married after all."

"That's what I just said," Saskia points out.

"Exactly," I say, rolling over in the grass to face her. I can feel it pressing against me, probably staining my shirt in the process, but I don't care. "I have to get Mom and Harrison to call off the wedding so we can move back here."

Saskia sits up fast, like she was hit by lightning. "That's it."

"It's genius, if I do say so myself," I say. "If it works, I'll be back in New York in time to start seventh grade in the fall."

"It's perfect. The escape plan starts now," Saskia says, and we shake on it.

This is it, I think as we slap our hands together. This is my way to make sure I can keep my home and everything I love about it. I just have to make sure the plan works.

CHAPTER THREE

The chocolatey smell of homemade cookies, still warm on the plate, fills Saskia's bedroom. Her mom made them for us as a special treat, since it's our last afternoon hanging out together. The school year ended an hour ago, and Mom will come by any second to pick me up and drag me to East Hammond.

We're using the time wisely. It's our last chance to finalize my escape plan. It's also my last chance to stuff my face with as many of Mrs. Stone's cookies as I can fit into my mouth at once before I leave for the summer. The way the chocolate chips melt perfectly on my tongue only add to the list of reasons why this plan has to work. I'm not prepared to give up even the smallest parts of my life in New York City. I want—*need*—to keep it all, down to the very last chocolate chip.

Saskia tilts her laptop so I can see her screen from where I'm sitting on her worn green armchair. She's opened her Notes app, where she's made a numbered list.

"Now, I have spent the last week doing some research," she tells me. "And I have found what the internet calls the definitive hallmarks of a good relationship."

I lean closer so I can read the words on her screen.

1. *Trust*
2. *Communication*
3. *Passion*

"Ew." I wrinkle my nose. *Passion* sounds like it means kissing, and the last thing I want to think about is Mom and Harristinks kissing.

"No time for ew," Saskia says, shaking her head. "Your mom said we could only hang out for half an hour, and we've already wasted half our time eating cookies."

My heart sinks. She's right. Mom only agreed to let me go over to Saskia's after I spent the whole week begging her, and even so, we only have half an hour before she comes to whisk me away. She's on her way right now with Harrison's car, which she had to borrow because we never needed or had space for one living in Manhattan.

Apparently, moving requires a "tight schedule."

Still, I'd never call time spent eating Mrs. Stone's cookies *wasted*. She really makes the best cookies on the planet.

"Now that we know this, we just have to come up with ways to ruin each one of these hallmarks," Saskia goes on. "If we can do that, they'll break up for sure. Let's start with passion."

"Ew."

Saskia rolls her eyes at me. "Passion is easy. You just have to ruin all their date nights."

"And how do I do that?" I ask.

"Stage an emergency," Saskia says. "Right when they get to their fancy restaurant or the movies or wherever, call them and tell them you got lost looking for a neighbor's cat, or you tripped down the stairs. It's easy to fake a limp. They'll have to rush home to help you, and boom. No more date night."

I nod, admiring her deviousness. "That's genius. Mom's always saying how her love language is quality time."

She says that's what makes family game night so important, for us to spend quality time together. If she can't get her precious time with Harristinks, maybe the love in their relationship will fizzle right up.

"Okay, now we need trust," Saskia says when she finishes typing up the plan for passion.

"We have to get one of them to spill a major secret," I say. "Something they weren't supposed to tell."

Saskia types *secrets* next to trust. "How do we do that?"

"I have no idea," I admit.

"Maybe Harristinks's kid will have some good dirt on him," Saskia says. "You should ask her."

"Linnea?" I bite my lip. "I don't know if I trust her enough to tell her about the plan." Besides, even if she did have the dirt, I wouldn't be able to hear her spilling it. That girl's voice could get carried away on a gust of wind.

Saskia types *ask Linnea for secrets* into the Notes app anyway. "She's probably just as annoyed that you're moving into her house. I bet she'd want to help. It's the best way to get dirt on Harristinks, so at least try to get a feel for where she stands."

"Fine," I say, even though the thought of bringing Linnea into something that's supposed to be just for Saskia and me makes my skin crawl. "I'll think about it."

"All right," Saskia says. "Communication."

I lean back into the throw pillows, letting the armchair swallow me whole as I think. I sit back up almost immediately, grinning.

"What?" Saskia says.

"Okay, you know how we're moving all of our stuff to Harrison's house today?"

"Yeah," Saskia says.

"I need you to make a phone call."

Saskia gives a nervous laugh. "What?"

I scrunch my nose as I try to remember the green letters painted on the side of the moving truck that came this morning to gather up all our furniture. "Long Haul Moving Company. I need you to call Long Haul Moving Company."

"Why?" Saskia glances at her laptop screen. "What does that have to do with the plan?"

"We just need to create a little miscommunication." I glance at the door, making sure that it's safely closed and no one can overhear us before I lean closer and whisper my plan. I'm barely finished explaining when I hear the front door of Saskia's apartment open, Mom's voice filling the space.

Saskia and I exchange panicked looks. This is it. Our last shared afternoon of the summer is over. And even though I know we have a plan, that I'll be back, I still feel like I'm going to cry.

"I'm going to miss you," Saskia says. Her voice comes out funny, like her throat is clogged.

Mine must be, too, because all I can do is nod.

"I wish I didn't have to go," I say, choking out the words.

"Me too," Saskia says quietly.

Her whisper makes my heart ache. I can't stand the thought of Saskia being so upset that she's this quiet, when her voice is normally the one that draws in the teacher from across the hall to ask our class to keep it down.

I cross the room as quickly as I can and pull her into a tight hug. She squeezes me back, her arms so tight around me that I can hardly breathe.

We let go when we hear our moms' footsteps coming toward the door.

"I should . . . go start the plan," I say, forcing a smile.

Saskia nods. She slams her laptop closed just as Mom swings the door open.

"Ready to go?" she asks me.

I want to shout *no*, but that won't accomplish anything. Besides, with the first part of the plan ready to go, I'll be back home in no time. So, with one last wave at Saskia, I follow Mom out of the apartment to the street, where she parked Harrison's car, ready to drive us away.

●●●

George gets the front seat, like always. I'm crammed into the back, a stack of cardboard boxes pressing up against my arm and a duffel bag stuffed under my feet. Our furniture and most of our boxes are piled into a moving truck, on its way to Harrison's house. Or at least, what the movers *think* is Harrison's house. But we still had to pile a few extra suitcases into every spare nook and cranny of the car.

We've only been driving for an hour, but it feels like we've been on this highway wasteland for a billion years. An endless stream of billboards flashes by.

George also won control of the aux cable—"No one wants to listen to Harry Styles for two and a half hours, Raisin Bran" (another insult cereal, for obvious reasons)—so I'm stuck with his whiny boy music blasting in my ears. Mom normally doesn't like it either, but she's too busy trying not to swear at the driver in front of us every time he forgets to use his turn signal to complain about the music.

I press my palms against the seat so I can lift myself up and cross my legs under me. My ankle smacks against the seat belt buckle, but it's still comfier to tuck myself away from the duffel bag full of my summer clothes. I hunch deeper in my seat, trying to take up as little room as possible, as if I could make myself disappear from this car entirely. Every roll of the tires takes me farther away from Saskia.

I glance at the front seat, where George taps his fingers against his knees along to the *Billy Elliot* soundtrack. Mom sits next to him, humming along as she drives even though she hates musicals. A big swell of frustration builds inside my chest. How can she be singing along so cheerily when she's right smack in the middle of ruining my life?

I remind myself of the plan to make myself feel better. If I want to get back home, Mom has to break up with Harrison. That shouldn't be too hard. He's the worst. Saskia and I didn't nickname him Harristinks for nothing.

It just might take a little bit of help from Saskia and me to show her how terrible he is. I pull my phone out of my pocket and text Saskia.

Autumn: Did you call?

Saskia: yes!!
Saskia: they said it "won't be a problem"
Saskia: totally bought it

I take a deep breath, close my phone, and go back to staring out the window. The sooner we get to Harristinks' house, the sooner I can put the rest of the plan in action.

Eventually, the stream of billboards lightens, giving way to thick rows of trees. I rest my chin on my knees. How far from New York is East Hammond, anyway? We've only been on the road for an hour, but the scenery outside looks so un-New-York-like, we may as well have driven around the world.

Mom turns off the highway, and we trundle through a few narrow and winding streets. Houses with cute shutters lining their windows flash by my window, leafy trees framing their freshly trimmed front yards. All of them have the same stiff, postcard-ready look. It's nothing like New York, with something new around every corner. Even though this town is tiny, I could get lost just by never being able to tell the houses apart.

"It's a bit of a detour, but want to drive through the center of town and see what it's like?" Mom asks.

I shrug. I want to get out of this cramped car and get

started on sabotaging the wedding, but I know Mom will end up doing whatever she wants. In this case, that means passing through the center of town.

We turn onto a little street lined with storefronts, a movie theater playing just two movies, and two restaurants with a few tables set up on the sidewalk. At the end of the street, there's a train station and a coffee shop.

"What do you think?" Mom asks as we turn down a second street that has a pharmacy and a post office. "Pretty nice, right?"

"Hold up," I say, sitting up straighter and craning my neck so I can see out the back window. The post office disappears from sight as we round a corner. "That was *it*?"

Mom looks at me in the rearview mirror. "It's a small town, Autumn. It'll be a nice change. You'll get to know it with Linnea and all your new friends."

I slump back down in my seat. There doesn't seem to be much to *get to know*.

But a few minutes later, the knotty feeling in my stomach grows a billion times worse. Because we pull up in front of Harrison's house, and Mom stops the car.

We're here. Our new "home."

When we park in the driveway in front of Harrison's house, which is just as prim as the others on the street, I glance around, looking for the moving truck. I don't see those big green letters anywhere. Perfect. I turn back to Harristinks and Linnea, who are waiting for us in the doorway. Their picture-perfect pose, standing there waving at us, gives me the creeps.

I drag myself out of the car, my sneakers crunching against the gravel driveway. The huge duffel bag bounces against the back of my knees as I trudge up the front steps.

"I'm so glad you're here, kiddo," Harrison says. He reaches down to hug me, but I don't move to hug him back, so he settles for an awkward shoulder pat before taking my bag from me. "I got this. Linnea, why don't you go show Autumn your room while we wait for the moving truck to get here?"

"What?" I gape at Linnea, my mouth hanging open. I realize, too late, that I'm being rude, and close it. "Are we sharing a room?"

Mom rolls up behind me with her wheely suitcase. "Don't be so dramatic, Autumn," she says with a sigh, as if I'm making too big a deal out of this fresh disaster. "There's two bedrooms between the three kids. It'll give you girls a chance to bond in your own space."

I bite the tip of my tongue to stop myself from taking a *tone* with her and getting myself grounded. That sounds like she lifted it right out of an article called

"10 Ways to Help Your Kid Bond with Her Stepsister" or something. I wish the hypothetical author had included "don't force them to bond in the first place" as number one.

Without saying anything, Linnea nods, her pale face going up and down, and turns back to the house. I follow her through the kitchen, which is so big it has space for a separate square counter in the middle of the room. Chairs are lined up around one end of it, and there's a second sink at the other. The windows reveal a backyard—a proper one with grass and a little swing set, like in movies. All my apartment in the city had was a fire escape I wasn't even allowed to go on.

"We can go out there later, if you want," Linnea offers when she notices me staring.

I jump, and nod without saying anything. I'm not about to admit that even one single thing about Harrison's house is nice. Not even all that grassy outdoor space.

Her bedroom is down a beige-carpeted hall to the left. Linnea's bed, neatly made with a striped duvet, has been pushed all the way against one wall to make room for my bed. I can see the imprints in the carpet where hers used to stand in the middle of the room.

Across the wall above the bed, she's strung a handmade banner, with *Welcome Home, Autumn* Sharpied across drawings of flowers. The words catch in my throat.

Home? This isn't home.

"I'm glad we're sharing," Linnea says, her voice so soft it barely breaks the silence.

I nod, not trusting myself to say anything. Mercifully, Harrison rounds the corner with my duffel bag and drops it at the foot of my bed.

"The movers just called," he says. "They're about five minutes away. Why don't you take a minute to get settled and then come join us outside?"

Linnea gives me a small smile before following her dad out of the room. I guess I should unpack a few clothes before the rest of the boxes pile into the room, but instead I sit on the edge of my mattress, tucking my toes under me so I can rest my forehead against my knees. The whole room feels like Linnea. I have no idea how I'm supposed to live here, surrounded by her music and movie posters.

Her bookshelf only has four books on it. The rest is stacked with sports trophies and participation ribbons. The walls are the kind of white Mom calls *off-white*, and there are a few posters of bands that Saskia would recognize, but I don't. Then I notice a half-open box on her desk overfilled with glossy printed photographs. The one on top is of Harrison and Linnea smiling with their mouths full of cheese puffs. It's cute—or it would be, if I weren't moving into this bedroom where I so clearly don't belong.

Tears build, hot and fast, behind my eyes. I blink them away. I'm not in the mood for crying. If I cry, Mom will overreact and flood me with non-solutions, telling me how much I'm going to love *getting to know* East Hammond and Harrison and Linnea. If I cry, it'd be like saying I accept this place as home enough to be sad about it.

And this place is not my home.

I jump off the bed and stride to the door. The moving truck will be here any minute—or, rather, not be here any minute—and that's when the plan will get moving. I cross my fingers hard in the pockets of my shorts. This *has* to work. This bedroom—this place where I so clearly don't belong—will not become my home. I won't let it.

When I get back to the porch, Mom turns to me with a bright smile.

"Linnea was just telling me that she's going on a bike ride with some of her friends tomorrow," she tells me. "You should join her."

"I don't know how to ride a bike," I remind her.

"Really?" Linnea asks, all shocked.

"There aren't many places for a kid to ride a bike in

the city," Mom tells her. "You could take your scooter, Autumn. It would be fun."

I sigh through my teeth. She's not the one who has to scooter all over East Hammond, so why does she get a vote on how fun it sounds? I can feel George staring down at me, the way he does when I'm being rude, so I fake a smile. "Can't wait."

"Hooray," Linnea says, throwing her skinny arms around my shoulders. I stiffen in shock. This is the most emotion I've ever seen her express. She drops her hands awkwardly back down at her sides. "Don't worry, I know there's not much on Main Street, but the best parts of East Hammond aren't in town. You'll see."

I'm rescued from having to come up with a polite response by the moving truck. It trundles down the road, exhaust sputtering loudly, and Mom beams when she spots it. The smile slowly fades from her face when the truck keeps driving. Straight past Harrison's driveway, down the road, until it's gone out of sight.

Inside, I'm doing a victory dance, complete with so much arm flailing it would poke someone's eye out if I did it in real life. It worked. The plan actually worked.

Mom stares at the truck with huge eyes, and Harrison's cheeks have gone pink and blotchy. I wish I could take a picture and send it to Saskia. *It's working.*

"What?" Mom takes a few steps down the driveway. "They must have to turn around for some reason."

But we wait a few more moments, and no truck appears. It's on its way to 302 Green Acres Road, right where Saskia told it to go when she called the moving company to claim that there had been a typo on our moving confirmation paperwork. It's a random house way at the end of Harrison's long street, almost half a mile away from his real address at 32 Green Acres Road.

Who knew all those times we spent doing our best impressions of our parents and teachers for laughs at sleepovers would actually pay off?

"There must have been some miscommunication," Mom says, glancing at Harrison.

I take a deep breath to stop myself from cheering. That's right. The communication here is just not working out. Phase one of the plan, on the other hand, is working perfectly.

"No, I definitely gave the right address," Harrison argues.

Mom runs her hand through her hair. "Well, obviously not, Harrison. I mean, honestly, this move has already been so hard. I asked you to do one thing and organize the movers, and this is what happens?"

Harrison's face turns pink and blotchy. "I'm sure I gave the right address. They're probably going to turn around and come right back."

"They'd be here by now if that's what was going on," Mom snaps. "We should go after them before all our stuff ends up lost."

"George, you're in charge," Harrison says, and he and Mom take off running for the car. They slam the doors shut and peel out of the driveway, going way too fast, to catch up to the truck before it disappears.

I watch them go, struggling to stop myself from smiling. My escape hatch is already springing open.

● ● ●

When Mom and Harrison come back, they don't seem to be in any better of a mood. Harrison's cheeks have gone from pink to full-on red, bright and shiny with embarrassment. Mom has that panicked look in her eye that she only gets when she's behind on a looming deadline for work or I bring home a particularly bad report card.

Guess that's an F– for Harrison. I cheer internally.

They've barely gotten out of the car when the moving truck pulls into the driveway behind them. The three of us—George, Linnea, and me—stand up when we see it rolling in. We spent the past half hour sitting on the front porch, making awkward small talk as we waited for our parents to get back. Even though they brought the moving truck with them, it's a relief to see Mom and Harrison so I don't have to listen to Linnea tell me more about our "super fun plans for tomorrow." Ugh.

"They somehow got the wrong address, and we had to fill out all this paperwork," Mom says when she reaches us, shaking her head.

"I'm sorry, honey," Harrison says, reaching over to squeeze her hand. "I don't know how this happened. There must be a typo on one of their spreadsheets or something."

"Well, we got everything straightened out in the end," Mom says, looking over her shoulder. Behind her, the movers have opened the truck and are easing Mom's favorite armchair out of the back. "We're lucky their office was able to flag them down before they ditched all our stuff at the wrong house."

Stupid office. At least Mom is annoyed with Harrison. Their communication is already off the rails, and the plan isn't even over yet.

The movers reach the front steps, holding the armchair between them. "Where does this one go?" one of them asks.

"Let me show you." Mom holds the front door open for them, and the little trio disappears into the house.

"All right," Harrison says, clapping his hands. "We got off to a rocky start, but let's get down to business. I'm going to show the movers where to bring in all the boxes. George, you're in charge of unloading the car. Girls, you're his assistants."

George leads us down to the driveway and pulls open the car door. He hands Linnea a light bag and holds another duffel out to me. I take it, but linger by the car, waiting for them to disappear into the house. As soon as everyone is safely inside and out of my way, I drop the bag on the driveway.

Now's my chance. Before any of them come back out, I jump into the back of the truck. It smells like cardboard and old paint on the inside, and there's barely any room to walk around. It's packed to the brim with boxes. Who knew we had so much stuff?

Mom got these stickers to keep the boxes organized. There's a row of boxes labeled *Kitchen* in her neat handwriting sitting next to two boxes with stickers that read *Master Bedroom.* I glance over my shoulder to make sure that no one's around, and then I peel a sticker off a kitchen box and one of the bedroom boxes. I scribble the right room for each box in pencil so that I can fix them later, and then I stick the wrong label on each box. I'm careful to put the stickers on the same spots on the box so no one will be able to tell that anything's been ripped off the cardboard. It takes a bit of rubbing down the corners, but the labels stick back on eventually.

When I'm satisfied, I get to work on the rest of the boxes. I stick *Kitchen* labels on boxes that are supposed to go to the bathroom, the basement, George's room. Mom will be unpacking spatulas in every room except the kitchen, and nothing makes her madder than a good organizational system gone wrong.

Let's see Harrison try to *communicate* his way out of this one.

I grin, wiping my hands against my shorts as I jump out of the truck. When I land on the driveway, I spot Linnea standing by the front door, arms crossed.

"Everything okay?" she asks.

I nod. "I was just looking for my, um, favorite book. But I don't know what box it's in."

"I'll help you look for it when we unpack the boxes," Linnea says. She turns back to the house, and I grab the duffel and follow her in.

As soon as I step through the door, I get why Mom was ready to cry as soon as something went wrong. Moving is total chaos. Everyone is running around, there are boxes everywhere, and it's about a zillion degrees out, making me instantly so sweaty from running around that my T-shirt is sticking to my skin.

Whenever I can, I sneak out of Mom's sight so I can peel the labels off. I have to get the right stickers back on each box before Mom notices the mix-up and figures out what I've done. I spend the whole afternoon on edge, jumping every time someone rounds a corner. I pretend to unpack a box when Linnea almost catches me, my heart hammering, but she only drops a duffel bag into the room and leaves again. Some of the labels are losing their stickiness after so much moving about, but I dedicate all the elbow grease I have to plastering them back on the right boxes. I barely make it to the last one before Harrison and the movers declare themselves done.

"That's all of it," one of the movers, whose sewn-on name tag reads *John*, says with a sigh.

"Thank you so much again," Mom says.

I drop into one of the kitchen chairs, fanning myself with my hand while Harrison walks the movers back to the door. Mom laughs when she sees me slumped over.

"Don't get too comfy," she says, ruffling my hair. "The boxes are in, but now we have to get everything out of them."

I groan. "Can't. Stand. Too. Weak."

I'm only being a *little* overdramatic. My arms feel like they're about to fall off after all the peeling-off-and-sticking-back-on I just had to do. Gluing on a label that has completely lost its stickiness takes some serious muscle, and my arms feel like limp noodles now.

"Come on," Mom says, pulling a pair of kitchen scissors out of a drawer. "The faster we get through it, the sooner we'll feel at home."

She cuts through the tape on the box closest to her, pulling the flaps open. The smile slides right off her face when she looks inside.

"What?" She pulls out a fluffy blue towel. "This isn't . . ."

She spins the box around to find her *Bathroom* label right where I put it back. She groans. "Harrison!"

He comes running into the kitchen. "What's wrong?"

Mom holds the towel up at him, and he blinks at her, confused.

"It looks very . . . clean?" he says cluelessly. I grin. He sounds like a complete dope.

"It belongs in the bathroom," she points out. "We are in the kitchen. Weren't you supposed to tell the movers where to put the boxes?"

Harrison sighs and crosses the room to pick up the box. "I'll take it over."

Mom takes the scissors to the next box, and I have to hide my smile behind my hand, because I know exactly what's about to happen. She opens the box and drops her head into her hands.

"Harrison!"

"What?" he calls as he comes back.

"None of this stuff belongs here." She lifts her head, her eyebrows all knitted together as she stares at the Christmas ornaments tucked in the box, which is clearly labeled *Basement*. "Do you think they're all wrong? I thought you were on top of this. It'll take so much longer to get it all unpacked now."

Wow, Harristinks. That's some really awful communication. I mentally fist-pump. The plan is going off without a hitch. Mom hates disorganization so much, she might be ready to call off the wedding here and now. Maybe she'll run after John and tell him to bring the truck to Harrison's driveway again, put everything back inside, and drive us all the way home. Maybe—

The sound of laughter interrupts my daydreaming. I look across the counter, and my jaw drops when I realize it's *Mom's* laughter.

She's laughing so hard, she doubles over. Harrison grins, wrapping his arms around her waist as he leans over to kiss her forehead.

Eww.

"This is just so ridiculous," she says, dabbing the corners of her eyes. "Could this move have gone any worse?"

"At least they didn't lose your favorite armchair," Harrison says.

Mom turns to hug him back. "That's true. Oh, let's leave the unpacking for tomorrow. We can get it done when the girls get back from their bike ride."

"Sounds like a plan," Harrison says with a big dopey grin. "What do you want to do tonight?"

"Order pizza," George pipes up.

Harrison laughs. "All right, I'll call the place right now. It's a shame it's so cloudy this evening, or we could have used my telescope to stargaze while we wait for it to get here. The sky is the best part of East Hammond."

Mom turns to me, her eyes bright. "Harrison is sort of an amateur astronomer. We'll have to do it another time. It's really the perfect welcome-home activity."

Sounds like a fancy way of saying he's a major dork, if you ask me. Which, of course, no one does.

"I'll go get her," Harristinks says, turning toward the closet. "Just to show you guys how she works."

His voice is so sappy, I'm starting to think he loves this telescope more than he loves my mom. Yet another reason this wedding is a terrible idea.

"How about we watch a movie instead?" Linnea says.

Harrison shakes his head at her. "My telescope is cool."

"Sure it is," she says, teasing, and Harrison laughs.

"All right, to the living room, which I bet is full of boxes that belong in the kitchen," he says, and Mom bursts into laughter again.

I follow George out of the kitchen, my heart sinking. I organized so many miscommunications, but the day still ended with a happily-ever-after for everyone but me. I force myself to take a deep breath. Saskia and I came up with a three-part plan. This was only the beginning. Just because this part of the plan didn't work doesn't mean it's over. I have way more ideas to throw their way.

Mom, George, and I will be back home where we belong before I know it.

CHAPTER
FOUR

For one glorious half second before I open my eyes, I think I'll see my own room, with its messy over-flowing drawers and a little window overlooking the honking cabs below. Then I remember, as my eyelids flutter open, that the only thing I'll see is Linnea's collection of posters.

Linnea is sitting on her bed. Not only is she already up, but her bed is also already made. Which is unfathomable. She's sitting cross-legged on the neatly tucked-in duvet, her earbuds in her ears. I close my eyes again so she won't see I'm awake and try to talk to me, but I'm a moment too slow.

"Good morning," she chirps, pulling her earbuds

out and dropping them on the little table that separates our beds.

I drag my eyes open, groaning. "Hi."

"Did you sleep all right?"

I shrug under the blanket. I'm not used to waking up with someone in the room. I have a whole routine for summer vacation mornings, and it involves burritoing myself deeper into my duvet, fluffing my pillows, and not talking to anyone for at least another half hour.

But now Linnea's staring down at me, fiddling with the end of her tightly wound braid as she waits for me to answer her question.

I wiggle out of the sheets and sit up, stretching my arms above my head. "I slept fine."

"It must be quieter here than in the city," Linnea says.

I nod. The dead silence last night freaked me out. I'm used to living way up on the seventh floor of a building, the lullaby of car honks and ambulance sirens flashing by below. Here, I stared out the window in the pitch-black, no streetlamps illuminating the street outside. Whenever a car drove by the house, an eerie glow from their headlights crept across the wall. My room in our high-up city apartment might have been noisier, but it never let the headlights in.

"Want to get some breakfast?" she asks, unfolding

her legs and leaping off her bed before I actually answer. "Dad said he'd make French toast, since it's your and George's first day here."

The prospect of French toast makes it a little easier to lift myself out of bed, but I cringe internally when I follow Linnea down the hall. She's already dressed and showered, and she's wearing jeans and a nonwrinkly T-shirt. I'm still in my pajama shorts and the baggy shirt I stole from George to sleep in. My hair is mussed up from thrashing all night, and my brain is too fuzzy from sleep to do anything about it.

"Look who's up," Mom says when we walk into the kitchen, her eyes lingering on my tangled hair for a minute, as if to remind me how much I don't fit in already. "Did you sleep well? I'm loving this quiet."

She takes a sip of her coffee. Harrison is standing behind the stove, sliding French toast onto plates. I hate to admit it, but it smells really good. My stomach rumbles, admitting it for me. I slide into a seat and take the plate that Harrison passes me.

"Lins, your friends still coming by later?" he asks.

She nods, mouth already full. "You're coming, right, Autumn?"

The last thing I want to do is pedal around East Hammond, especially with girls I don't know, when I need to spend the day calling Saskia. She's always been better at planning than me, and I bet she's come up with more ideas for getting Mom away from Harri-stinks so we can go home.

"I still don't know how to ride a bike," I remind them.

"Take your scooter," Mom says. "It'll be good for you to get out and see the town."

I sigh. We normally spend summer vacation Satur-days at a museum, which I used to think was super boring, but anything sounds better than scootering around East Hammond, even if it means standing around and looking at the same painting for a zillion years. But I guess spending the day with Harrison is more important to Mom now.

I stab a forkful of French toast. "Guess I'll go get ready, then."

● ● ●

Turns out, bikes can go *way* faster than scooters. Lin-nea and her friends are already at the end of the street. I slam my foot against the pavement, hurtling my scooter up the hill, but even with my little wheels trun-dling as fast as they can against the road, it's not fast enough to keep up. The only thing making me feel bet-ter is that I don't have to wear a dorky helmet.

The girls stop at the intersection ahead, and Linnea circles her bike around, speeding back to me. She slows her pace, matching mine as she pedals.

"We gotta teach you to ride a bike," she says with a grin. I guess something about being in her element must take away her shyness, because I can actually hear her for the first time.

I struggle to huff some air without letting her see how out of breath I am. "I'm all right."

She eyes my orange handlebars. "You sure? It's, like, a ten-minute ride to the park."

That sounds like absolute hell, especially since the armpits of my T-shirt are already getting damp with sweat, but admitting defeat now and turning back would be way too embarrassing. I nod, slamming my foot into the road again, and push off after her.

She pedals back to her friends, who are waiting with one foot against the road to balance their bikes. The tallest one, who I'm pretty sure is named Katie, starts pedaling again as soon as I reach them.

East Hammond is just as boring up close as it looked from the car window. The streets are lined with trees, broken up by same-looking houses, and a car drives by us only once every few minutes. The most exciting thing we pass on the way to the park is a woman jogging by in the other direction. By the time we get there, my lungs feel like they're going to fall out of my butt and my T-shirt is covered in sweat. I fold my arms across my chest, praying it keeps the sweat stains hidden from the other girls. They're out of the dorky helmets, walking alongside their bikes as they push them by the handlebars, leaving me as the only disheveled one of the bunch. I flap my shirt a few times when they're not looking, desperate to dry out, and hurry to catch up.

The park looks just like the rest of East Hammond, except without the houses. There's a big plot of grass with a dirt path winding through it, and yet more trees surrounding us. I push my scooter down the path after the other girls. We head toward the outskirts of the trees. Linnea and her friends swing their kickstands down to prop up their bikes. I let my scooter drop into the grass and move to help them with the blanket Linnea's friend Erica brought for the picnic, but they already have it set up by the time I join them. I sit on the edge of the blanket, tucking my knees under me, while Erica passes out the Fluffernutter sandwiches.

"I didn't know you were coming," she tells me apologetically, handing Katie and Linnea aluminum-wrapped sandwiches.

"Oh no, that's totally my fault," Linnea says, her pale cheeks flooding with bright red embarrassment.

"It's fine," I say quickly.

"Have half of mine," Linnea says, tearing hers apart. I shake my head, about to tell her it's really fine, but she shoves the smushed white bread into my hands. I take a careful bite, the Fluffernutter sticking to the roof of my mouth as I chew.

"You still owe me a truth," Erica says to Linnea. She's already done with her sandwich, which she ate in two frighteningly huge bites.

Linnea blushes. "I'm not telling you who I like."

I squirm against the picnic blanket. Watching them makes me think of Saskia and the easy way we tease each other, and then I miss her so much my heart aches.

"Come ooooon," Katie whines. "I told you I like Jamie Wellerstein!"

"And I told you I like Grady Roper," Erica says.

"And I don't have to tell you anything," Linnea argues.

I shuffle into myself on the blanket, trying to make myself as small as possible. If I can shrink enough, maybe they'll forget I'm here. A soft breeze kicks up around us, carrying the sweet smell of cut grass.

"That's how the game works," Erica sputters. "You can't just back out of answering." She turns to me, and I shrivel even more. "Okay, Autumn, you have to side with me here. We played Truth or Dare at our last sleepover, and Linnea picked truth and then refused to tell us who she likes. That's cheating, right?"

I rub the back of my neck. On the one hand, that's definitely cheating. On the other, I've never had a crush, and Saskia's the only other person I know who still doesn't *like* anyone. I don't want them to find out I'm a crush-less weirdo and make fun of me. Silence might be the best policy here. "I guess not."

"See? I knew she'd agree with me," Linnea says.

"Fine, well, if you won't make her tell us," Katie says, "then you have to answer for her."

My heart drops to my stomach. "I've never heard that rule before."

"That's because I just made it up," Katie says, grinning. "Did you have a boyfriend back in New York?"

"No," I say. No one in my grade had a boyfriend, not really. Steph Decker went out with Andrew Johnson for a few months, and some people took dates to the end-of-year dance, but that was it. A few of the other girls were jealous of Steph, but I've never so much as glanced twice at any of the boys in our grade.

Should I have a crush on a boy? All these girls seem to. Most of the girls in my grade did too. But I always thought it was okay that I didn't, because Saskia never did either.

The ten trillion questions firing through my brain

must show in my eyes, because Katie raises her eyebrows. "Well, do you like anyone?"

"No," I say. "The boys in my grade are super weird."

This is not technically a lie, I tell myself, thinking about the time Andrew got a bunch of the boys to have a hot dog bouncing competition in the cafeteria at lunch. The teachers on lunch duty were not happy—though, in his defense, some of the hot dogs bounced disturbingly high.

"There must have been at least *some* cute ones," Erica says.

I pause, mentally thinking through the boys in my grade. "No. No cute ones at all."

"Okay, well you must have had a crush at some point," Erica says, tossing her hair. "I'm the dating expert of the grade."

"It's true," Linnea tells me. "She was the first one to go on an actual date."

Erica nods. "Kyle Fellman took me to the frozen yogurt place in town at the end of last year, and I think we're gonna go to the movies together sometime over the summer. So I can help you figure out the crush situation."

"I've never had a crush," I admit, and Erica gapes at me.

"*Never?*" she asks, staring at me like I've just

sprouted four heads and all of them started talking in a different language at the same time. "Not even once?"

"Not even once," I say, folding my arms across my chest. Dating expert or no, Erica can't tell me what's true about my own life.

"What, so there's never been someone you really want to hang out with all the time?" Erica says.

I think of Saskia. "Well, obviously."

"Someone cute?" Erica asks.

Saskia's cute. I've always thought so, anyway. Her nose scrunches up in this funny way when she's laughing, and it always makes me unable to take my eyes off her. I nod without saying anything.

"Okay, well, does being around this *someone* make you feel all bubbly and happy inside?" Erica asks.

Saskia always makes me feel like that. Like someone's shaken a can of soda and popped it open in my chest.

"Yeah," I say quietly.

"And do you think about this special someone all the time?" Erica goes on.

I do think about Saskia a lot. Before I found out I had to move to East Hammond, I thought about what adventures I could plan for us, what silly notes I could pass her in language arts before we got phones and could just text each other, what matching bracelets

I could get her for her birthday. Now that Mom has dragged me here, I think about when I can call her next, or what she might be up to right now, how her summer camp is going.

I nod.

Erica leans back, smirking. "Then you've had a crush."

I stare at her. I do not have a *crush* on Saskia. Saskia is my friend. My best friend. Crushes are for boys.

But no boy has ever made me feel the way Erica described. I've never spent loads of time thinking about any boy. Definitely no boy has ever given me any kind of warm fuzzy feelings.

"I don't have a crush," I tell her, but the girls just laugh.

"Sure sounds like you were thinking of a special someone when I was asking you all those questions," Erica says. "Tell us about him."

My tongue feels like it's been tied into a tight knot. I can't move it to form any words. Because the special someone, as Erica insists on saying, isn't a *him* at all.

What is that supposed to mean?

Can I have a crush on a girl?

I want to ask someone, but the only person I can think to ask is Saskia, and I obviously can't tell her about *this*. Ever since Mom started dating Harristinks, she hasn't been around as much to talk to about stuff like this. George would probably tease me—in a funny way, but still not helpful.

I glance at Linnea. I could tell her. But my whole plan is to get *out* of East Hammond, not get closer to Linnea.

She sees me looking at her and gives me a small smile. "Guys, let's talk about something else. Autumn can tell us all about this mystery crush when she wants. When do you guys think we'll get our schedules for next year? I want to see how many of the same classes we're in."

Katie and Erica eagerly start talking about the foreign languages they signed up for, leaving me to give Linnea a grateful smile. My plan is still to get out of this town as fast as possible, but I'm grateful that she rescued me from Erica's and Katie's questions.

After everything Erica said, I have more than enough of my own questions to answer for now.

CHAPTER
FIVE

The first thing I do after dinner is take a shower to wash off the scooter sweat sticking to my skin. The second is call Saskia.

I hide in Linnea's room, my dripping hair still wrapped tight in a towel I borrowed from the linen closet, and dig through my bag until I find my phone. Settling onto the bed, I hit CALL and take a bunch of deep breaths. The room smells like cardboard from all the half-unpacked boxes scattered across the floor.

The phone rings three times before Saskia picks up. "Autumn?"

The sound of her voice makes me nervous. I can't stop thinking about Erica's questions. *Does being around this someone make you feel all bubbly and happy inside?*

I'm trying to test my feelings for her, but I can't figure them out. How am I supposed to find the line between a friend and a crush? Can she be both?

"Hi," I say, my thoughts too muddled to come up with something more interesting to say.

"How's the escape plan going?" she asks.

"So far, so blech," I say. "Mom thought the moving mix-ups were hilarious."

"What?" Saskia screeches. I pull the phone away from my ear before she goes on. "How could she think they were funny? Your mom is like the most organized person I've ever met."

I sit on the edge of my bed, watching water droplets trickle down my legs. "I know. I can't believe it."

"We have to move on to trust, then," Saskia says. "Have you talked to Linnea about the plan yet?"

"No," I admit. "I'm still not sure if she'd go for it or not. She made me a Welcome Home poster."

"I bet Harristinks made her," Saskia points out.

"Maybe you're right," I say. There's footsteps in the hall, and my heart sinks. We've barely gotten a chance to talk, and I haven't figured out my confusing fizzy feelings at all. So much for testing Erica's crush theory. I lower my voice. "I have to go. Talk soon?"

"Of course," Saskia says.

I hang up just as Linnea enters the room, crossing over to the dresser to pull out her sweatpants. The sound of Saskia's voice should've made me feel better. It always does. But this time, Erica's crush questions flooded into my brain as soon as I heard her, and now it's all I can think about.

The swirl of feelings in my stomach reminds me of the week before winter break when I was in third grade. A bunch of fifth-grade boys got in trouble for running up and down the halls singing, "Make the Yuletide *gay*" in these really sarcastic voices. When a teacher told them to stop, one of them turned around and shouted, "What? It just means happy." They ran away laughing, and the teacher chased after them to give them detention.

I didn't get why they thought it was so funny, or why they got in trouble, so I told Mom about it after school.

"Why was the teacher so mad?" I'd asked her.

"Gay has two meanings," Mom had explained. "In some contexts it means happy. Like in that song, they're singing about making the Yuletide a happy time. But that meaning is a bit old-fashioned these days. Now it means . . ." She'd glanced at me, with an odd look in her eyes, like she was searching for the right words.

"Some boys fall in love with other boys. That's what those kids were joking about, which wasn't nice of them at all. We'll talk about it more when you're older."

Well, I'm older now, and I've met loads of gay men since then. Mom's best friend, Uncle Jordan, got married to his husband, David, last summer. But even though I'm older now, I'm suddenly too afraid to ask Mom about it. Because what if some girls fall in love with other girls too? What if *I'm* one of those girls? What if Erica is right, and all the feelings I have for Saskia add up to a crush?

"Thanks for sticking up for me today," Linnea says, and her voice jerks me out of my thoughts.

I look up at her. "Of course."

"I didn't want to tell them about the guy I like," she says quietly. She closes her dresser drawer and sits on her bed opposite me.

That gets me burning with curiosity, but if I ask her about her crush, she might ask me about mine, and there's no way I'm about to tell her about Saskia. Not before I figure it out for myself.

"You should have told them that," I say instead. Saskia and I never tease each other about stuff that we genuinely don't want to talk about. Boundaries are boundaries.

The familiar red blotches creep over Linnea's cheeks as she thinks over what I've said. "Oh, I don't know."

"Why not?" I ask. "They're your friends, right?"

"Yeah," Linnea says quickly. "I just . . . I don't . . . um . . . I don't like confrontation, I guess."

I stare at her. "Confrontation?"

"Yeah, just . . ." Linnea trails off, staring at her shoes. "It's lame, I know. It just feels easier to go along with it, you know?"

I do not know. I've never been a *go along with it* kind of person. That's why I came up with this plan in the first place, why I'm so ready to fight Mom tooth and nail on this stupid move—even if she's not willing to listen.

"You should stand up for yourself," I tell her. "Be bold. If they're your friends, I'm sure they wouldn't be mad."

Linnea shrugs. "I guess. I'm going to help Dad and your mom unpack."

"I'll come help as soon as I find some clothes in these boxes." I scratch my arm, uncomfortable in the prickly silence between us. She nods and shuts the door behind her.

I jump off the bed, digging through my duffel bag until I find my comfiest T-shirt.

Maybe Saskia's right, I tell myself as I pull it on, my wet hair dripping down the back. Linnea can't be happy that I'm here, taking over her room and the space at the kitchen island. I bet she wants me to get out of her house just as much as I do. And I bet she knows how to push Harristinks' buttons way better than I do.

Maybe I should tell her about the escape plan.

The thought makes me a little nervous. She could just as easily tattle on me and ruin the whole thing. But the plan would work so much faster if both of us were in on it.

We have to spend the rest of the evening unpacking, which means there's going to be nothing but chaos until we go to bed. I'll think about it later, I decide, and I leave the bedroom to help unpack.

CHAPTER
SIX

I t takes us the rest of the week to finish unpacking. It feels nice to wake up in a room that doesn't smell like days-old cardboard, even if I resent being a single step closer to "settled in" to Harrison's house.

I roll out of bed after Linnea, as usual, and stumble to the kitchen for breakfast, where Mom greets me with a suspiciously large smile.

"What's up?" I ask as I open the fridge and pull out milk for my cereal.

"I have some fun news," she says in a tone that makes me think this news is only going to be fun for her.

"What is it?" I ask, splashing milk over the Honey Nut Cheerios I picked out for breakfast.

"Well, I was thinking about how you seem to be struggling to adjust to East Hammond," she says, and I perk up. Maybe she's actually noticed how miserable I've been for our entire first week in East Hammond, and we'll be on our way home by the end of the day. Anticipation bubbles in my stomach like the sip of champagne Mom lets me have at New Year's. "And I think I found a way to help you feel more at home here."

The bubbly feeling falls flat.

"What do you mean?" I ask.

"I signed you up for Linnea's tennis camp," she says, her smile growing impossibly wider. "The counselor said you can start today."

I stare at her. Tennis?

No thank you.

"C'mon," Mom says. "Isn't this great? You'll meet some friends. And you'll get to spend more quality time with Linnea."

The last thing I'm worried about is more quality time with Linnea. I already share a room with the girl. How much time does Mom think I need?

"Do I have to?" I ask, and Mom's shoulders deflate like a popped balloon.

"Yes, Autumn," she says. "It'll be a good thing for you."

I sit down and scoop a mouthful of cereal into my mouth. "Okay," I say when I swallow, because I don't see how I can get out of this now. "I will go play tennis."

Mom ruffles my hair as she passes me on the way out of the kitchen. "Great, sweetie. I think you'll love it."

Given that I've literally never played tennis before, whereas Linnea has a whole trophy shelf, I have some serious doubts about that.

● ● ●

Dana, who is Linnea's camp counselor, has short brown hair pinned up in a ponytail and wide shoulders. She swings her racket, demonstrating something (I've already forgotten what it's called) for us. The racket doesn't fly out of her fingers the way I'm sure it will when it's my turn to try. She gives us a thumbs-up, and something about her makes me want to impress her, even though I know that's a doomed effort. There's no way anyone is going to be impressed with my tennis skills.

"All right, let's have a few volunteers try it out," she says.

Linnea's hand flies into the air, and when Dana

points her racket toward her, Linnea grabs my hand and drags me from the sidelines onto the court.

"Okay, girls, you ready to demonstrate the backhand?"

I give her a tiny nod. I'm not even remotely ready to attempt whatever type of swing she's trying to get me to do, but she's also really cool, and I don't want her to think I'm lame.

"All right," she says. "Show us your stuff, girls."

Linnea tosses the tennis ball up in the air, and she does it so perfectly, she looks almost as impressive as Dana. I gulp. How long has she been doing this?

She brings her racket down with a crack, and the ball flies over the net toward me. It's spinning way too fast, and it's already so close—too close—it's going to hit me before I have time to even swing my racket.

I squeal, and duck.

My cheeks burn as I hit the green-splotched ground of the tennis court. There's a smattering of giggles from the sidelines, where the rest of the girls are huddled under a spot of shade by the fence, and then a shushing noise. I straighten, shooting Dana a grateful smile. She nods back at me, and I flush.

"Hon, is this . . . your first time ever playing tennis?" Dana asks, jogging over to me.

I nod. "I mean, I played once in gym . . ."

She laughs. "You should have said! Here, swap places with Hannah"—she gestures for a lanky blond girl to come over—"and watch how she does it. Don't worry, we'll make a Martina Navratilova of you yet."

I scurry back to the shade, cheeks still flaming. I don't know who Martina Navratilova is, but at least Dana doesn't think I'm pathetic.

She seems really impressed with Linnea, though. She tells us all to watch Linnea's careful movements. I stare at her muscly arms, but I don't see what Dana's pointing out. At the day camp Saskia and I used to do together every summer, we stuck by the crafts table. In fourth grade, I taught myself how to knit and made her a lumpy hat that she wore all winter until the seams unraveled, while she painted me a self-portrait. I don't know a thing about sports. Why couldn't Mom have signed me up for the arts group we passed on our way through the Y instead?

When Linnea and Hannah finish demonstrating, Dana gathers us all around. "Okay, it's time for our lunch break, and afterward, we'll all partner up and practice serving. Sound good?"

I nod, because lunch always sounds good, especially if it comes instead of playing more tennis. As Dana leads us to a cluster of picnic tables on the lawn by the courts, Linnea falls into step next to me.

"I didn't realize you've never done this before," she says, and I blush. Between this and the bike riding thing, Linnea must think I'm stupid. It's not my fault that my best friend and I prefer hunting for the best ice cream shops to running around a hot court.

"We should be partners after lunch," she says. "I can help you. If you want," she adds, color rising into her pale cheeks.

"Thanks," I say. It might be nice to not embarrass myself in front of her again. I've done that enough this past week.

Besides, I think as I watch her slide onto one of the benches at the picnic table closest to us, scooting over to make room for me next to her, I need to find a way to bring up the escape plan. Bonding over tennis could help.

She smiles. "Cool. It'll be fun."

We pull our sandwiches out of our paper bags.

"How do you like East Hammond so far?" Linnea asks.

I sigh as I unwrap my sandwich. "It's all right. I miss New York, though."

A warm breeze rustles the grass under our feet, and I close my eyes as it sweeps across my face. The lawn must have been mowed recently, because it smells like sweet fresh-cut grass.

"What do you miss most about it?" Linnea asks.

I think of Saskia, and for a moment I wonder if I should tell Linnea about her. But then I remember all of Erica's questions. What if Linnea can see right through me? What if she realizes who my *special someone* is as soon as I mention Saskia?

"My friends," I say vaguely. "And . . . I had all these plans for the summer I never got to do."

"Like what?" Linnea asks. She's still smiling at me, resting her pointy chin in her hand, looking up at me with her eyebrows raised, like she cares what I have to say.

It makes me want to keep talking to her. I never would've thought I'd feel this way around Linnea, but the eagerness with which she keeps asking questions as if she truly cares about the answers makes me feel comfy around her in a way I never expected.

"I just love finding new spots. Places I've never been before. It's . . ." I pause, racking my brain for the right words. "Like this one time, I'd planned for us— me, I mean—to go to this pop-up museum that was all about ice cream, because"—I catch myself before I mention Saskia's love for ice cream—"well, because it sounded fun. And on the way, we—I—found this tiny tea shop with all these adorable mugs and I got one shaped like a fox and it's one of my favorite things I own." I take a deep breath. "And then I knew New York a little better."

Linnea smiles. "We could do stuff like that here."

I sigh, staring past her at the tennis courts lined just past the grass. Two middle-aged women have started a game on one of the courts, and Dana jogs down the hill to tell them that our camp has the space reserved.

"It's not the same," I tell Linnea. "The city is my home. When I go on adventures there, I get to know it *better*. That's the whole point. That's actually why I want to get out of here."

Linnea frowns. "What do you mean? You're moving in. Here to stay."

"I have a plan." I glance over my shoulder to make sure no one's listening, and lean in across the table, lowering my voice. "I want to get my mom to break up with your dad."

Linnea's jaw drops. She stares at me, silence hanging between us.

I rush to keep talking. "That way, I could go back to the city. Back home. And you'd get your room back, your life back. You wouldn't have to spend your whole bike ride with your friends looping back to make sure I didn't get lost."

I leave out the part about how much I need to get

back to Saskia. The part about how much I hate Harri-stinks, how much better my mom could find. Those things won't convince her, obviously.

All I can do is pray it's enough.

"But—" Linnea's eyes are still wide when she meets mine.

"You should help me," I say quickly. I cross my fingers under the table, so hard it almost hurts. If she tattles instead of joining me, the plan is ruined. I'll be doomed to stay in East Hammond forever. And probably be grounded the entire time.

Linnea's just staring at me, her eyes so wide that they're practically popping out of her face, blotches of red appearing on her cheeks. "You want me to . . . help you? With this plan to break up our parents?"

It's my face getting hot now. My heart hammers hard in my chest, each beat getting wilder and wilder the longer I go without saying anything. I open my mouth, tripping over my tongue as I try to find a way to backpedal. She clearly doesn't want anything to do with this plan, and if she blabs, it's all over for me.

"I mean . . . what? No. I was just kidding. I . . . um—" I shift my weight on the bench, the splintery wood digging into the backs of my thighs.

"I mean . . . ," Linnea says, cutting me off. "I guess . . .

I *have* always wanted my parents to get back together. And if Dad marries Sasha, that'll never happen. But I don't know about this."

"Be bold, right?" I remind her, crossing my fingers hard under the table. *Please, please, please—*

"Okay," Linnea says, staring down at her food. "I'll help you. Maybe it's the push Dad needs to get back together with my mom. Tell me about your plan."

I breathe a sigh of relief, even if I can't help the confusion swirling through me. A second ago, she was reacting to my plan like I'd just dumped bird poop into her sandwich.

"Are you sure?" I ask.

"Yeah," Linnea says, finally meeting my eye. "Be bold, right?"

I nod. She's in. She won't tattle on me, and I have an ally. Someone to fight alongside me in East Hammond until I can get back to New York and Saskia, my usual ally in all things. I look over my shoulder and spot Dana coming up the grassy hill to wave us back to the courts.

"Later," I say quickly as we get up to throw away our trash. "We can have a planning session."

Linnea nods, and we shake on it as we follow Dana down to the courts for the afternoon practice.

CHAPTER
SEVEN

I t's only been a little over a week since I talked to Saskia, but it feels like it's been a hundred years. An eternity, even. Stars have been born and have died since our last phone call. But between unpacking, and then tennis camp, and the handful of calls she hasn't answered, it's been impossible to find a second to myself. So the moment Linnea leaves for breakfast in the morning, I pounce on my phone to call Saskia.

"Your idea was great," I tell her as soon as she picks up. "I talked to Linnea a few days ago, and I got her to join the plan. With her help, it'll work even faster, I bet."

"That's good," Saskia says, her voice suddenly sounding far away.

"How's camp going?" I ask, sitting on the edge of my bed. If Mom had never met Harristinks, if I were in the city where I belong, I'd have started camp with Saskia last week. Right now, I'd be putting on my blue camp T-shirt and rushing through breakfast so I could make it on time for morning board games.

Instead, I'm busy being thankful that I finally have a day off from tennis camp. The first few days were grueling. I can feel every muscle in my body, and not in a good way.

"It's going great," Saskia gushes. I smile, picturing her in her camp shirt. I wish so badly I could be there with her. "I made a new friend. Her name is Delilah and she's *so* funny. Yesterday she told this joke—"

Saskia's voice keeps coming through the receiver, but her words blur together. She's made a new friend. A new friend who sounds way funnier than me.

I'm stuck in East Hammond, wondering what it means to have a crush on a girl, if *I* might have a crush on a girl, and the whole time, Saskia's just been replacing me.

"She sounds great," I say.

"She really is," Saskia says. "I should get going. I don't want to miss—"

"Morning board games," I finish for her.

I listen to the beep on the other end as she hangs up, suddenly feeling more alone than ever.

● ● ●

"We should get out of the house for our first planning session," Linnea says. She's joined me in her bedroom, where we've planned to have our first brainstorming meeting to talk about the plan since I recruited her earlier this week. I've already shut the door to her bedroom and propped a pillow in front of it so it'll flop over and warn us if anyone's trying to sneak in. But when I point to it, Linnea shakes her head.

"I don't want anyone to overhear."

"Okay, well, where should we go?" I ask.

Linnea grins. "It's a surprise. Just pack a bathing suit, okay? I'll ask your mom if we can bring some snacks."

She skips out of the room, leaving me to change into my red suit and pull my T-shirt back on over it, curious in spite of myself.

"Where are we going?" I ask again as Mom waves us out of the house. I know there's a pool at the Y, since we walked past it on our way to the tennis courts before camp. But Linnea just shakes her head.

"It's a little bit of a walk, but I don't want you to be stuck scootering the whole way."

I smile gratefully. My thighs ached for three days after propelling my scooter to the park, eons behind her friends on bikes. Linnea may be quiet, but she notices all the little things. And then acts on them. It makes me more excited to spend the whole day hanging out with her. Saskia and I are both loudmouths who get in trouble every day for talking in class. We've learned to listen to each other while we both talk at the same time, so our conversations are noisy and overlapping, a mish-mosh of our voices that no one can understand but us. Linnea's quiet tone and rare words made me think she was annoyingly shy, but now that I see the way her brain works behind all her silence, I think I like her.

"Thanks." Even though I want to get away from her town as fast as possible, I think it might be nice to be her friend. "So where are we walking to?"

She shakes her head at me. "Nice try. Just follow me."

There's no sidewalk lining the roads, except for the streets in town, so we walk on the side of the road. Our flip-flops clack against the pavement with every step. Every few minutes, a car flashes by us, and we hop from the road to the grassy stretch of dirt between the concrete and the trees. More often than not, Linnea waves at the driver.

"How do you know everyone?" I ask after a blond woman waves at Linnea through her windshield.

"Mrs. Schumacher?" Linnea asks, glancing over her shoulder at the silver Toyota disappearing over a hill. "She's Nilah's mom. A girl in my grade."

"Aren't there like a million people in your grade?" Mom told me that almost every kid in the town goes to the same school, and even though the town isn't big, that's a lot of kids. My school in the city only has twenty kids in my class.

Linnea laughs. "Yeah. But that's normal. I mean, everyone in the whole town goes to the same school. Except for a few kids who go to private schools in Norwalk, but they all still come to our dances and sports games and stuff."

I blink at her. I can't imagine walking down the street and just knowing the names of people I pass by.

"So everyone just knows everyone?" I ask.

"Not exactly," Linnea says. "I mean, there's people in my grade I know better than others. But I'm the student council president and the head of a few clubs at school, so I get to know everyone pretty well."

As if to prove her point, she waves to what looks

like a high school boy walking his dog on the other side of the street.

"I didn't realize you were the Queen of East Hammond," I tease.

"Excuse me," Linnea says. "President. I was elected, thank you very much."

The laugh that bubbles out of my mouth surprises me. Who knew Linnea had a sense of humor?

We keep walking, and even though it's less sweaty than scootering, I could use a break from these hills. And these trees. They seem endless, lining the road for as far as I can see. It's kind of nice, though. Like the buildings in the city, only there's space between them, and the greenery is kind of pretty. A warm summer breeze swooshes through the leaves, and I'm filled with the sudden urge to spin into it.

"What are you doing?" Linnea asks, staring at me as I stretch out my arms into a twirl, my bag bouncing against my hip bone as I do. I crane my neck backward, and I can see the whole sky.

"There's just"—I sigh—"so much *space* here."

Linnea nods. "The city was so intimidating when I went there to visit you guys."

Maybe that's why she was always so completely silent whenever she came to visit. Linnea lights up now that I know her in her own element.

"Someday, I'll take you around the city," I promise. If we're going to be friends, she'll have to come visit me sometimes after Mom and I move back home. "You'll see, it's the best place in the world."

Linnea laughs. "I mean, Broadway is cool and all, but East Hammond is the best place in the world."

I politely refrain from rolling my eyes. Don't get me wrong, it's nice to have so much space, but . . . no one writes songs about East Hammond for a reason. It's just trees and concrete and tidy houses and—

We round the bend, and Linnea throws her arms out in front of her. "Ta-da!"

—and water.

The road ends, the concrete fanning out as it meets a dusty stretch of sand. And beyond that, the ocean. Sunlight bounces off each little wave as they tumble over each other, packing down into the wet sand on the shore.

"I didn't know there was a beach in East Hammond," I choke out.

Linnea pulls me to the sand. I follow her, running faster as the first few grains of sand dribble onto my flip-flops. The sunbaked sand scalds the bottom of my feet.

"Oh, hot," I say, bouncing onto my toes.

Linnea pulls me closer to the water, where the sand

is a bit cooler, and pulls two towels out of her bag. She tosses me one and stretches the other out on the sand in front of her, jumping onto it as soon as it settles. I mimic her, and my feet scream in gratitude as I hop off the sand.

"Isn't it the best?" she says, looking out at the water.

I nod. New York has beaches, too, but we have to take the subway for over an hour to get there, and they're always packed full of people. There are a few people here today, but there's enough room for us to stay way spread out, and we have a huge section of the beach all to ourselves. I inhale deeply, and all I smell is the clean, salty air washing up from the water.

"All right, this is pretty nice," I tell Linnea, and she smiles.

"Just wait until you get to the summer fair," she says. I tilt my head, and she goes on. "It's this really cute street fair that happens in town every summer. All the best food, plus all the stores do super-fun activities. The whole town shows up."

Her voice lights up when she talks about her town, and suddenly, I get it—why she's really helping me. We're the same. She understands what it's like to love a place, to know it all the way down to its core. She's found where she belongs in East Hammond, her little corner of her community, just like I have in my corner of New York, and that's why she gets how important it is for me to make it home.

"You'll see, the fair is the best," Linnea finishes.

I swallow my *ugh*. The last thing I want to do is stick around in East Hammond long enough to see the summer fair, but I don't want to tell her that and make her feel bad about her home.

"When did your parents get divorced?" I blurt to change the subject.

Great. Smooth one, Autumn. Nothing like a nice chat about divorce to cheer us up.

"A couple of years before Dad met Sasha," Linnea says. I blink. It's weird to hear Mom called by her actual name instead of Mom or Ms. Sinclair.

"Oh wow, so do you remember it?" I ask.

She nods.

"My parents have been divorced as long as I can remember," I say. I cautiously stretch my feet into the sand, burrowing my toes underneath it. The buried sand is cooler than the scalding layer on top. "George always tells me it was not fun."

Linnea shrugs. "It was all right. It was the stuff that came before that was not fun."

"Like what?" I ask.

"They just fought, like, all the time," she says. "It's way better now that they each have their own house.

93

My mom lives in Stamford. I go see her every other weekend."

I swallow, my throat suddenly thick.

"My dad lives in California," I say. "He got married and he moved there. I spent a summer with him a couple of times, when I was little. But mostly me and George stay with Mom."

"That sucks," Linnea says, and I nod. "It must be nice to have George, though. I've always wanted— Well, it just seems nice."

I smile in spite of myself. "Yeah, he's pretty cool. He's going away to college in the fall, though. Tufts."

"Is that far?"

I turn to look at her, squinting as the sun hits my face. "Massachusetts."

Linnea's nose wrinkles. "That sucks."

"It does," I say. I used to look forward to having Mom all to myself after he left. Mom used to spend every spare minute she had with me. We had this one game where we'd go for a walk, and we'd try to find a new bookstore or a store that sells something so inexplicably random, and whoever got there first won. My best win was the time I found a teeny-tiny store that sold nothing but cool buttons. The diamond-shaped blue one I picked out is still tucked safely away in my memory box.

With George at Tufts, I figured Mom wouldn't be able to ditch me every weekend. We could go back to our exploring. There's a paint-by-numbers shop I found three blocks from our apartment that I've been saving for the next time we play our game. But instead, here we are in East Hammond, like she couldn't bear the thought of living in an apartment with just the two of us rattling around inside.

"Anyway, we should plan," I say. "So far, all I've tried is messing up the moving plans."

Linnea laughs. "That was you?"

"Yep," I say, grinning proudly. "I also planned to ruin one of their date nights, but I'm not sure how."

"Okay, well, what if we pretend one of us is super sick?" Linnea suggests.

The thought makes me smile. Mom has been ditching me for *date night* for two years. I want nothing more than to ruin one.

"Oh," Linnea adds, slapping my arm. "We could start tonight. Dad said he wants to cook dinner, and he *hates* when things go wrong in the kitchen. You should say you want to help him."

"Perfect," I say. Bringing Linnea into the plan was the best idea.

Linnea props herself up onto her hands, flashing me a smile. "Race you to the water?"

She takes off running across the sand. I tear off after her, the hot sand burning the bottoms of my feet. She beats me to the waves, and she splashes a spray of salty water in my direction as I jump in after her.

I dive under the next big wave that rolls up toward the shore, and stay under as long as I can, the movement of the waves rocking me. It's not exactly silent underwater, what with the sound of the waves crashing, but it's like white noise drowning out the rest of the world. I keep my eyes screwed shut, salt prickling my eyelids, seeing how long I can last until my lungs feel like bursting. I kick my feet downward, digging them into the soft, wet sand, and stand up, sputtering as I inhale. Another incoming wave knocks me over, and I let it drift me toward Linnea.

"It's nice here," I tell her, and for this moment, the water cooling me down as the sun rays shatter the sky overhead, I mean it.

● ● ●

Harrison is a bossy chef. Every time I reach for my phone to see if Saskia has answered the text I sent her half an hour ago, he clears his throat.

"No screens in my kitchen," he says.

I make a big show of sighing. If there's anything I've learned since Mom got me a phone halfway through sixth grade, it's that nothing grinds adults' gears more than a kid who spends too much time on their phone. Even if those same adults spend their whole day typing away on their own screens.

Harrison seems like one of those adults. So I spend another second on my phone before putting it back down on the counter. He shakes his head at me, frowning, and I know I've succeeded in annoying him.

"Okay, we're going to make our own tomato sauce," he says.

"Sounds hard," I say, sighing. The vein in Harrison's forehead twitches, which I'm starting to learn means I'm getting under his skin. If I want the evening to end in a fight between him and Mom, I need him as on edge as possible by the time his dinner goes up in smoke.

"Can you open this can for me?" he says.

I know how to open a can, but instead I pick it up and stare at it. "How?"

Harrison opens a drawer and pulls out a can opener. "Okay, so you line this up—"

As he shows me, I reach for my phone again. Saskia has answered my text, so I swipe open our messages.

> **Saskia:** camp was good!!
>
> **Saskia:** sorry I took forever to answer, I was having ice cream with Delilah

Reading her words gives me a queasy feeling, my stomach roiling as the smell of canned tomatoes hits my nose. I wonder if she takes Delilah to our table in the corner of our favorite ice cream place, ordering mint chip. Our favorite. The thought makes the sick feeling worse, like waves getting bigger before they hit the sand.

"Are you paying attention?" Harrison snaps.

I jump. I'd forgotten about the can. The vein in his forehead is really jumping now. I put my phone down.

"It's confusing," I tell him, and he sighs.

"I'll just open the cans if you can watch the garlic there," he says, pointing to the pan. "Tell me if it starts looking brown."

I go to stand by the pan. There are only a few cloves of garlic sizzling in the pan, but the kitchen already smells amazing. I stare at the oil as it bubbles around the chopped garlic, making it bounce just a little. No matter how good the kitchen smells, that sick feeling keeps rolling around in my stomach, like it's having a quiet temper tantrum. I can't stop thinking about Saskia. Delilah and Saskia.

Am I jealous?

Erica didn't say anything about jealousy, but I can picture her asking about it. *Does it make you jealous when this special someone finds a new best friend?*

Harrison interrupts my thoughts with a yell.

"Autumn," he says, pushing me out of the way to reach the pan. "The garlic is burnt. I told you to watch it."

I look down at the pan. The edges of the garlic are black, and the thick garlicky smell has turned to charcoal in the air.

"I was," I say.

"I'll have to start over here," he says, pouring the crisp garlic into the garbage.

"How can I help?" I ask, and his forehead vein dances a jig as he turns to me.

"How about you just watch for today," Harrison says. "We'll work our way up to having you help."

I shrug. "Okay."

I jump onto the counter next to the stove, swinging my feet as I watch Harrison put fresh garlic into the oil. In a minute, the kitchen smells good again.

"How about after dinner we try out my telescope?" Harrison says.

I glance at his telescope, which is still set up by the window. If I'm being honest, it sounds pretty cool.

The stars are much brighter in East Hammond, where there's no building lights and streetlamps between us and the sky. But Harristinks is sure to ruin the pretty views by droning on and on about space history or something.

"I guess," I mutter to hide my interest.

"It's the best," he says, his whole face lighting up. "I got that telescope just after Linnea was born. The stars have always been my favorite thing, and I wanted her to grow up sharing that."

I tune him out as he rambles on and on about what kind of telescope it is and how it works. I knew he'd find a way to ruin the stars.

Harrison coughs, staring at me expectantly, and I jump, realizing he's just asked me something.

"Can you get me the salt?" he says, the annoyance in his tone making it clear that he's repeating himself.

He has three containers lined up on a shelf: one each for salt, sugar, and flour. Obviously, I hand him the sugar instead. He doesn't realize until the tomato paste is coated.

"Autumn," he says, his voice so quiet it sounds like a whine. He turns off the heat and pinches the bridge of his nose, closing his eyes and taking a deep breath. He opens them, turning to look at me. "How would you feel about ordering pizza?"

"Great," I say, jumping off the counter. "Extra pepperoni for me."

Before he can answer, I skip out of the kitchen, an extra bounce in my step as I think about how sick Harrison is of me. The plan is unfolding exactly as I hoped it would.

●●●

"I have an idea," Linnea says, bursting into her room. I look up from the book I'd been reading.

"We should have a picnic," she says. "Dad hates eating outside. It'll make him even more annoyed. Come help me."

She grabs me by the hand and pulls me out of the room, pushing a checkered blanket from the linen closet into my free arm. We run outside and spread the blanket out over the grass. She smooths the corners, making sure the blanket lies flat, and leads me back inside.

"Help me carry the telescope," she says. "We gotta be careful. Dad will freak if it gets damaged."

I might want to annoy Harrison, but even I'm not evil enough to want to destroy something that matters so much to him. We each take one end, walking slowly as we carry it outside. It's heavier than it looks, and I

101

watch my step carefully as we set it by the blanket outside. Linnea surveys our work with her hands on her hips and gives a satisfied nod.

"Perfect," she says, turning to me. "Thanks for helping."

"Of course," I say. With any luck, Harrison will get bitten by a mosquito and make his bad mood even worse. I can't believe it, but Saskia was right: bringing Linnea into the plan was genius. It's already going so much better with her input.

The pizza gets here, and Linnea leads everyone outside to the picnic we set up. Mom beams as she settles on the blanket between me and Harrison.

"This is so sweet, girls," she says. "Thank you both for doing this."

I grin at her, but shoot Harristinks a worried sidelong glance. It's actually pretty nice out here, and I don't want him having too good of a time. The moon has already risen even though it's still pretty light out, and there's a warm breeze that floats through the evening air.

"Great work, Lucky Charms," George tells me as he grabs his own slice. "I was craving pizza."

I smile at him. "You're so welcome for ruining dinner."

Harristinks sighs, but bites into his pizza instead of

saying anything. I grin. His annoyance is practically vibrating the air around him.

"I have to say, this is lovely," Mom says. "So, girls, how was your day?"

"We went to the beach," I say, surprised by the enthusiasm in my voice. "It's so much nicer than Coney Island. It's huge and there was basically no one else there and the water is so clean."

George laughs. "Is that some joy I detect in your voice?"

I can feel Linnea's gaze burning into the side of my face. She's waiting to hear my answer. Lying would help the plan more, but I don't want to hurt her feelings. And I *did* have a really good day.

"Yeah," I say. "Yeah. We had a good time."

I turn to smile at Linnea, and she grins back at me.

"How's your preparation going?" Mom asks George. "Did you do your summer reading?"

"No," George says with a laugh. "I will be doing that at the very last minute."

"That sounds like a great plan," Linnea says. "I'm going to do that with the summer reading list too."

"Now, look at your influence," Mom says to George, shaking her head. "Is this the way you want your stepsister to see you?"

George turns to Linnea, looking her up and down. "Do you think I'm cool?"

She shakes her head mischievously, and I give her a high five. Our hands slap so hard, the sound echoes through the yard.

"Bullied," George says, crossing his arms over his chest. "I'm being bullied."

I know I'm supposed to be ruining the picnic, dragging down the mood so Harrison stays annoyed with me, but I can't help myself. There's something nice about all of us spread out over the blanket, the jokes we trade traveling way further than they did when it was just George and me.

We eat as the sun goes down, warm summer night falling around us.

"Is it dark enough to do some stargazing?" Mom asks as she reaches for a napkin.

Linnea jumps up, wiping her fingers on her jeans. "Can I show Autumn how it works?"

Harrison walks across the picnic blanket on his knees. "Let me set it up for you."

It's a long process, with lots of looking in the small end of the telescope and adjusting the angle little by little. He handles the telescope so gently it's almost reverent. It really is his favorite thing in the world.

Eventually, he waves me over.

"Take a look," he says, a note of pride in his voice.

I bend down, closing one eye and pressing the other into the end of the telescope. When I see the stars, I gasp. They're so bright—much brighter than I've ever seen them in the city. It's beautiful. I find myself wishing Saskia were here, so I could show her. She loves Van Gogh, and his *Starry Night* painting.

The stars look tiny, even through the telescope, but I know they're actually burning as big as the sun, a million billion miles away. It makes me feel so tiny, but in a good way.

The same way living somewhere as big as the city made me feel tiny. Even though everything around me was huge, I felt like I belonged to something. Like I was a little part of something much bigger than just me. Me, my family, our home, Saskia, my school—each of our little pods connecting together to make something as huge and beautiful as the city we all lived in. So even though we were all just a tiny piece of it, we grew it into something that mattered because of how much each of us loved our home.

I guess the stars are kind of like that too. Tiny, a billion miles away, but still burning so bright it makes them matter.

"My turn," George says, pushing me out of the way.

"Hey," I protest as I hit the ground. I throw myself back on top of him, but he's heavier than me, and I barely manage to make him budge away from the telescope. And then Linnea piles on top of us as we wrestle for a chance to look up at the stars.

CHAPTER
EIGHT

I whip out my phone before Dana turns my way, pos-
ing with my racket, and snap a selfie to send to Saskia.
She responds with a string of heart eye emojis. They
send a flurry of nervous butterflies through my stomach. Erica would definitely say that's a crush feeling.

I quickly drop my phone into my bag as Dana circles back over to us. We're supposed to be practicing
our serves. So far, I've served all my balls straight into
the net. Except for the one that bounced by my feet and
hit me in the face instead.

Linnea's still laughing about that one.

"Let's see what you've got, Sinclair," Dana says
to me.

I bite my lip. The last thing I want is to make a fool of myself in front of Dana. Given that I've been coming to tennis camp for almost a month now, I've lost the "total newbie" excuse, and my serve is still just as pathetic as it was on my first day.

Taking a deep breath, I toss the ball above my head. Watching it carefully, I pull my racket back and swing it forward, and—

Miss the ball entirely.

It falls straight back down to the green-painted court, bouncing uselessly off to the side. My racket swings all the way forward, pulling me into a stupid-looking half-twirl. My cheeks get hot as I feel myself blushing. On the other side of the net, Linnea hops around in a victory dance.

Dana bites back her smile. "Okay. That was—"

"You can say it," I say. "It was a disaster."

"Yeah, that was not good," she says with a laugh.

"This time, keep your eye on the ball, and rise up to meet it a little sooner," she says, tossing me the ball.

I catch it with one hand and toss it back up again. I keep my eyes on it as I swing my racket forward, and this time, my racket actually hits the ball. And sends it flying into the net.

Dana gives me a high five anyway. "Progress. Nice work."

I beam as she walks away to gather everyone for the end of the day.

After we finish packing up our stuff, I follow Linnea to the parking lot, where we wait for Mom to pick us up. Across the lot, Dana weaves her way through an aisle of cars, pausing when she reaches a little red one. She leans against it, waiting.

I watch her, wondering if I should go over and thank her for her help today, when a blond girl with short hair runs up to meet her. I think they're going to hug, but instead, the blond girl pulls Dana toward her. They're holding both hands when they kiss.

I gasp. Dana and the other girl get into the car and pull out, but I can't stop staring at the spot where they were. Something about it makes my throat tighten, as if it's trying to squeeze tears out like the last few squelches of toothpaste at the bottom of the tube. I blink fast, but I can't stop thinking about how casually they held hands. Like it's something they do all the time.

It must've started with a crush. I wonder if Dana thought about the blond girl, the way Erica says people with crushes do. If she got butterflies and wanted to hang out with her all the time.

Just the same as I do with Saskia.

Is that where a crush leads? Hand-holding? More?

Is that what I want?

Linnea calls my name and I spin on my heel to see she's already a few feet away from me.

"Your mom's here," she calls.

I look over my shoulder one last time, but Dana and the blond girl have already disappeared down the road.

●●●

Harristinks planned his first date night with Mom since we moved here for tonight, but even though it's finally time to sabotage, I can't get my head in the game. My brain has been stuck on the image of Dana and that girl in the parking lot since yesterday, my thoughts picking it over like a particularly itchy scab.

Mom gets all dressed up for date night, and I'm sure Harristinks does his best, though I still think he looks like a turtle. He's just proving my point: they don't belong together.

"George is in charge," Mom says as she slips her shoes on by the front door. I shoot him a look, and he tosses his hair at me. "And there's an emergency number on the fridge."

The emergency number is the key to Linnea's and my plan. If we stage an emergency, Mom and Harristinks will have to come rushing home. Their night will be ruined and their tensions will be running high, the perfect recipe for sapping the passion out of their relationship and creating a huge fight. Just like Saskia and I planned.

"Have a good time," I say with an insincere smile as they leave through the door.

As soon as their car rolls out of the driveway, I turn to Linnea. George has disappeared into his room, where he spends most of his days FaceTiming his friends as they prepare for college together, leaving Linnea and me to plan alone.

"Well," I say, glancing at my phone to check the time. "We should time our emergency so they get our call after they get to the restaurant and order, but before they get their food."

"Ooh, it would be perfect if we call just as their food is coming out," Linnea says with a giggle.

I picture Harristinks' face when he finds out he has to rush home right as his food is dropped in front of him, and I laugh too.

"Okay, so let's give it another twenty minutes," I say. "That gives us time to come up with the perfect emergency."

Linnea's face shifts. "Twenty minutes?"

"Yeah," I say. "So we get them right when they get their food?"

"That's just . . . soon," Linnea says, her nails between her teeth.

I purse my lips at her. "Be bold, remember?"

"I don't think we thought this through," Linnea says. "This just feels an awful lot like a confrontation."

"It was your idea," I protest.

"It seemed funny, but now that we're actually doing it . . ." She trails off, but the rest of the sentence is in her eyes. Now that the time has come to go through with the plan, she's too scared.

"We have to do this," I tell her, my voice breaking. "We *have* to."

"Or we could just . . . order a pizza," Linnea says, getting up. "I have to pee."

A likely story. She just wants to escape this conversation.

She disappears into the bathroom, leaving me to sort through the take-out menus in a kitchen drawer, looking for the pizza place we ordered from when we had our picnic. I sift through the menus, frustration rumbling in my fingertips. Linnea's meekness is about to be the death of my plan. How am I supposed to convince this girl to step up when she's scared of her own shadow?

I've just found it when Linnea walks into the kitchen, her face beet red.

"What's wrong?" I ask.

"I, um . . ." Linnea swallows, her face growing impossibly redder. "We might not have to fake an emergency after all."

"What happened?" I drop the menus back into their drawer, moving toward her.

"I just got my period," Linnea says. I'm about to tell her that doesn't count as an emergency when she adds, "My first one."

I gasp. She has perfect timing.

"I got mine a few months ago," I tell her reassuringly. "I can help. But you're right. We should call my mom. Here," I say, passing her the house phone, "you call her and I'll go find a pad for you."

Linnea dials with a shaky finger as I dash off to the bathroom to grab her a pad from my stash under the sink. I rush back to the kitchen to hand it to her. Her fingers curl around the plastic wrapping as she talks into the phone.

"Thank you," she says quietly. Her face is still red when she hangs up. "They're on their way home."

As soon as she gets the words out, she buries her face in her hands.

"It's not embarrassing," I tell her, putting my hand on her shoulder. "This is normal. Natural," I add, remembering what our health teacher told us back at

113

school. We learned all about periods in fourth grade, and at the time my whole class thought it was uncomfortable and hilarious all at once. But then half the grade got their periods over the next couple of years, and it just felt normal.

"I'm the first of all my friends," Linnea whispers.

Saskia was the first in our grade. I remember the beginning of fifth grade, her face as red as the stain on her jeans. Being the very first made it harder, but we all rallied around her. I dug through the lost and found until I got the cutest pair of pants in there for her to wear the rest of the day, and another one of the kids in our class brought her a cookie at lunch. By the end of lunch, she was lording it over us all, bragging about her cramps.

I put my arm around Linnea's shoulders. "You're not the first of your friends. I told you, I've had mine."

She gives me a small smile, wrapping her arms around my back, and before I know it, we're hugging.

The front door bangs open, and Mom rushes in. I spring away from Linnea before she sees us hugging and makes a whole thing about how well we're getting along.

"How are you feeling?" she asks, putting her arm around Linnea. "This is such an exciting day. Do you know how to put that on?" She nods to the pad in her hands.

Before Linnea can answer, Mom starts explaining how the pad works, unfolding it and handing it to Linnea.

"Thank you so much," Linnea whispers, gratitude written all over her face. "You're the best."

"Of course, honey," Mom says, wrapping her arms around Linnea's shoulders.

I glance at Harristinks, hoping he's annoyed. Maybe he'll be mad that Mom called off the date night and doesn't want to go back out.

Instead, he's watching her help Linnea with huge eyes, a small smile on his face, like she's the greatest, most beautiful person he's ever seen. It almost makes me like him, for a second. The way he clearly sees that my mom is one of the most awesome people on the planet.

Almost.

● ● ●

Linnea's been asleep for ages, but I keep tossing under the sheets. How can she rest at a time like this? All of my best efforts come crashing down around my ears. No matter how hard I try to start a fight between our parents, every day ends with them still in love. Disgusting.

Frustrated, I kick the sheets off and plop down at

the desk instead. I pull out a fresh piece of paper and start sketching an outline of East Hammond. Maybe if I can see the plan laid out in front of me on a map, I'll be able to see where I'm going wrong. I label Harristinks' house where I've been annoying him nonstop, the Y where Linnea joined the plan, the beach where we had our first brainstorming session. After a moment of hesitation, I add the park where Erica bombarded me with crush questions. It's not related to the escape plan, but it still feels important.

I lean back when I'm done, staring at the drawing. I've gotten to know East Hammond pretty well, I realize. I've made memories all over this map.

And yet, I still don't know what's missing. What more I need to do for my plan to work.

I get back into bed, where I toss and turn for the rest of the night.

CHAPTER
NINE

I hate to admit it, but Linnea was right: the East Hammond summer fair is pretty great.

Every store in town—which is way more than you'd think given that *town* is only two streets—has decorated their storefronts with huge flowers and colorful fairy lights. They have booths set up on the sidewalk, and the street is closed to traffic, instead filled with games, food carts, and an actual bouncy house. The whole street smells like flowers, roasting barbeque, and fried Oreos.

My first thought is to follow the spiced smell of empanadas to its source, but then I spot a bouncy house towering at the end of the street.

"Am I too old for that?" I ask, pointing to it, and Linnea shakes her head.

"No way."

Harrison tries to call us back, but we pretend not to hear him as we take off running. I climb in after Linnea, and we jump around for all of three seconds before I trip over my own feet and slide down, taking Linnea down with me. We fall into a heap on the balloon-y floor, laughing.

Mom appears on the other side of the netted walls, arms crossed. "Do you two mind? Harrison wants us to all go get lunch together."

"I'm not hungry," I say, laughing as I struggle to get to my feet, only to have Linnea use me as a pole and send us both tumbling back to the floor. We burst into laughter as we collide again.

"Get out of there this instant," she hisses, pointing to the flap leading out of the bouncy house.

Swallowing, I exchange looks with Linnea, and we walk/fall our way back to the sidewalk. Mom takes our hands, leading us back through the maze of booths and food carts.

"Your dad has a lot of things he wants to do today," she tells Linnea before giving me a stern look. "It means a lot to him that we stick together, okay?"

"What if we want to do kid stuff?" I ask, giving the bouncy house one last yearning look.

Mom gives me a tight smile. "You can do whatever you want later this afternoon, okay? Right now, let's have some time together. That's what this summer is all about."

I trudge after her. In my opinion, we've spent more than enough time together. We've already been in East Hammond for just over a month. How much time do we need before Mom leaves me alone?

Linnea rolls her eyes at me, and I grin back, but the smile slopes off my face as we reach Harrison. She's *my* mom. Who is Linnea to complain? Harristinks is the reason we have to go back in the first place. I can always count on him to ruin anything and everything.

"Shall we get lunch?" Harrison says.

Linnea raises her eyebrows. "Snack run?"

"Time starts now," he says, handing her a $10 bill.

Linnea grabs my hand and runs, pulling me toward a food cart.

"What are we doing?" I ask as she orders a funnel of fried Oreos from the cart.

After pocketing her change, she turns to me. "Snack run. It's me and Dad's tradition for the summer fair. We see who can get the most and best snacks for ten dollars, and then the haul is lunch. Oh, and we only have ten minutes, so hurry."

Before I can so much as taste a fried Oreo, she drags me to the cotton-candy stand, and then the corn dogs. We're down to our last dollar when I realize we don't have any drinks.

"We will keel over of dehydration without at least some water," I say, eyeing the amount of powdered sugar already coating Linnea's hands.

She rolls her eyes. "You are not at all getting the spirit of snack run."

I glance at my phone. "We only have a minute and a dollar left. What else can we do?"

"Lemonade?"

I grin. "Way better than water."

I hold our full-to-the-brim cup of lemonade and two of the corn dogs as carefully as I can as we run back to the meetup table. Linnea slides into one of the seats, slamming the case of Oreos victoriously onto the table.

"Beat that," she calls out to Harrison, who comes running up with Mom.

He smirks as they unload plates of funnel cake and a bucket of kettle corn bigger than my head onto the table. Seeing all the food heaped up like that, a giant pile of processed sugar and deep-fried goop, makes my stomach turn a little.

I can't wait to shove it all in my face.

Linnea starts arguing that she deserves the win when George saunters up. Smirking at us all, he drops a tray lined with fancy mini tacos in the middle of the table.

Linnea stops talking, eyeing one topped with a heap of fresh guacamole. "Okay, yeah, George wins. Where did you even get these?"

He plops down next to me, snatching a shrimp taco before I can get to it. "A winner doesn't share his secrets."

Linnea purses her lips at him, and I frown. First she rolls her eyes at my mom, and now she's teasing my brother? Just because Harrison is here for family time doesn't mean she gets to lay claim to *my* family.

I smile up at George. "Thanks, Froot Loops."

"No problem, Honey Bunches of Oats," he says, slinging an arm around my shoulders.

Grinning, I snuggle closer to his shoulder and take a taco.

"I, for one, feel like we're all winners here," Harrison says as he helps himself to a corn dog.

George and I exchange looks. We're way too competitive for that garbage.

"Not in the snack run," Harrison adds. "I won that, obviously. But we're all here, sharing a meal together, and that brings me so much joy."

His sappy words make me want to barf even more than the fried grease I've just scarfed down way too fast.

He's not done, though. He takes Mom's hand, smiling at her. "Which makes it an extra special time to share some news. We've decided to get married in mid-August." He squeezes Mom's hand, and it's like he's squeezing my stomach, too, the way it rolls over and threatens to make me hurl. "Which means we're going to spend the next month in full wedding-planning mode. A big fun family effort."

The word *family* sends my head spinning. We're not a family. Just because Mom decided to fall in love with Harristinks doesn't make him my family. No amount of wedding planning can change that.

"Can I help with planning?" Linnea asks, wiggling in her seat.

I glance at her. This whole family thing would make her my sister. I was down to be her friend, but her *sister*? I barely even know her. And besides, I already have a sibling. George is the world's greatest older brother, even if I'd never admit it to his face. I don't need to sacrifice everything—my home in New York, my school, summer camp, *Saskia*—just to get a second sibling I never asked for and don't need.

"Of course I want you all to help," Mom says. "In

fact, I need all your help. We're so excited we got a date this soon. I can't believe we were able to get something this quickly, but that means we only have a month to get everything done!"

I gape at her. A *month*? And she sounds excited about this unmitigated disaster. What is she thinking?

"We have a cake tasting coming up next week," Mom says, fishing through her purse for a slender notebook with a floral pattern on the cover. The inside is full of notes, and it's bulging with business cards from photographers, florists, bakeries, and venues.

"And I'll be there to sample every bite," George says. "Even though I already know the chocolate will be winning."

I stare at George, but he doesn't notice. I don't understand how everyone else has jumped aboard the family train. George barely knows any of these people, either. Is cake really all it takes to make a family?

If family is enough to make me give up everything, there has to be more to it than that.

"We also have to get dresses, confirm the venue, choose floral arrangements . . . There's so much to do, and so little time." Despite the horribleness of her words, Mom smiles hugely as she snaps the notebook shut. "I'm so excited. I just can't believe how fast we're making it all happen."

Linnea gets up to throw a stack of greasy napkins in the trash, and I get up to follow her.

"Are you excited for cake tasting?" Linnea asks as she dumps the napkins. "I seriously can't wait. I've never even been to a wedding before."

I stare at her, confused. "Me neither."

"I know this means our plan failed," Linnea says, slumping her shoulders. "But at least we get some cake and a party out of it."

I tug at the end of my ponytail. Not even cake can fix this loss. East Hammond is cuter than I thought it would be, and there are more places to explore hidden away than I ever imagined. I like Linnea so much more now that we've spent all this time together, now that I understand she's quiet because she's busy noticing things—like how I'm not as excited as everyone else. Even Mom hasn't bothered to notice that part.

But just because I don't hate East Hammond doesn't make it home.

"The plan's not over," I tell her. "We just have to change it up a bit. Sabotage all the wedding planning. If everything goes wrong, they're going to blame each other and end up calling it off."

There can't be a wedding if they can't plan a wedding, after all.

"That's what we thought would happen when we ruined their date night," she says, her lip twisting.

"We have to keep trying," I tell her. "We just have to."

She stares at me for a long minute. "Okay."

We head back to the table, and I spend the rest of the day turning wedding planning sabotage plans over in my head. There's no way I'm letting them get married at the end of summer. They can't.

● ● ●

Mom spends dinner gushing about the cake tasting tomorrow. George is just as excited. I can barely even look at him. I know the wedding doesn't matter as much to him, seeing as he's ditching me for college at the end of the summer anyway, but he could at least pretend to care about the fact that my life is falling apart.

"You like maps, right, Autumn?" Harristinks asks me as I help Linnea clear the table after we finish eating.

I nod slowly. I don't want to share any piece of myself with Harristinks, even if it's something as small as a hobby.

"I thought so," he says. "I found that map you drew of our neighborhood while I was unpacking."

"Oh, you mean the one I drew to plan my summer?" I ask as snarkily as I can manage. "Thanks."

Harristinks rubs the back of his neck. "I want to show you something I think you might like."

I slump behind him as he leads me to the ancient desktop computer set up at his desk. He sits behind it, and I stand awkwardly behind his chair, watching the computer as it takes approximately one thousand years to turn on. The monitor is the only thing making any noise. I can't think of a single thing to say to Harristinks.

"I just saw how much you enjoyed the telescope," he says, "so I thought you might enjoy this."

He pulls up a wizened computer program that takes even longer to open. When it finally loads, my eyes widen as I lean toward the desk in spite of myself.

It's a map of the stars.

Thin silver lines connect constellations, creating delicate drawings that dot the inky background. He scoots his chair to the side.

"You can toggle to have a look around," he says. "I thought it could be fun to draw our own."

"We can do that?" I ask, leaning closer to take in the pixel constellations. "Map the stars?"

He nods, sliding a large piece of paper across the

desk. "I found some instructions online to do a basic model. Want to get the telescope and try it?"

Spending time with Harrison is the last thing I should want to do. I should be running in the opposite direction, far away from this man who wants to pretend like he's my dad. Especially now that he's trying to rope me into his ridiculously nerdy hobby. Instead, I find myself nodding.

It turns out even the most basic star map is technical work. We start by drawing a circle on a large rectangular paper, and then we have to measure out lines to get the right angles and degrees. Harrison spews a bunch of his best science teacher facts as I trace light lines across the circle with a ruler, and some of them are maybe not even that boring. I'm starting to get why he's so obsessed with space that it's practically his entire personality. When we're done setting up the map, Harrison pulls up a website where we can see what the stars look like tonight. I carefully connect the constellations onto the map. My favorite is a little one I've never heard of called Aquila.

"It's named after the bird that carried Zeus's thunderbolts," Harrison tells me when I point it out to him. "Want to go try and find it?"

I nod again, and he leads me out to the backyard, pausing in the kitchen to pick up the telescope. He carries it so carefully out to the grass that it makes me paranoid just to watch him, worried it could slip out of his grasp too easily.

"Okay," he says, sitting in the grass and pointing to the stars. "See that bright one right . . . there?"

I sit next to him, not super close, but near enough that I can follow the direction his finger indicates.

"That one?"

"That's Alistair," he says. "It's the brightest star in the constellation. And then from there, you can trace it." He moves his finger along, showing me the arrow-like shape of the star-flung bird.

"It's pretty," I say quietly.

Pretty doesn't really do it justice. Staring up at the sky, I wish I could tuck myself in with the lightning bolts, let the starry bird carry me along with them until it crossed over New York, bearing me gently home. It occurs to me suddenly that I could see the same constellation in the city. Maybe if Saskia looked up right now, she could see it too. Aquila, soaring over both of us, reminding me again of how tiny I am under it. Tiny in a way that matters, though, like each little star makes up the bigger picture.

"Want to take a look at it through the telescope?" he asks, nodding to the eyepiece.

"I do," I say, and I shuffle over to take a look.

CHAPTER
TEN

I catch Mom admiring her ring when I get up for breakfast the next morning. She's just standing there in the kitchen, a steaming mug of coffee in her right hand, her eyes glued to her left. I clear my throat when I walk into the kitchen, and she jumps, pink splotching into her cheeks.

I don't tease her about it, though. I have more important things to talk about. I barely got any sleep last night, because I was too busy staring at the stars outside my window. The stars weren't visible at all from my bedroom in the city. The streetlights washed away any hope of seeing the inky sky. Last night, though, it felt like I could see them all. And even though I'm barely awake right now, all that lack of sleep blurring my vision, I want to talk to Mom about Saskia. Ever since we got to East Hammond, she's only become more distant. Harder to reach. She barely even answers my texts anymore.

Mapping the stars is all well and good, but what's the point if I can't share it with my best friend?

"Good morning," Mom says brightly as I hop into one of the kitchen island chairs. "I have a job for you today."

"I actually wanted to talk to you about Sas—"

Mom sighs, as if she can tell where the rest of my sentence is going, and my voice fizzles out mid-word.

"I want to hear everything you have to say, but can it wait until later?" Mom says. My face falls, and she talks even faster. "I know you miss your friend, but we have so much to do here to get everything ready. The wedding is happening so much sooner than we thought! I need you to spend some time today think-ing about what kind of dress you might want to wear to the wedding. We have fittings soon. And I thought some dance lessons for you and Linnea could be fun?"

"But I just want—"

But Mom is already draining the last of her coffee and setting her mug in the sink. "I have to drop you off at tennis camp a bit early today so I can make it to my appointment with a potential photographer on time. Go get ready, okay?"

And she breezes out of the room as if I never said anything at all.

●●●

I pace around the edge of my bed. Four steps between every phone ring. Three if I take big ones. Thirty-two steps, and the ringing stops.

Hi, you've reached Saskia. Just text me. I never listen to voice mail!

I recoil in shock. Voice mail? I know for a fact her day at camp is over. I got home from tennis over an hour ago.

She must be with Delilah. Her new best friend.

"Hey, it's me," I say, cringing at the awkward sound of my voice talking to no one. "Mom and Harrison are getting married at the end of the summer. We're starting wedding planning tomorrow." I breathe in again, slowly. "I just miss—"

The machine beeps.

"What?" I say, lowering the phone to stare at the screen, but the automated voice is already back on to tell me that I'm out of time. I fling my phone onto the bed. It thuds against the mattress, giving the most un-satisfying little flop.

I should call back. Finish telling her how much I miss her. But my stomach is in knots at the image of her seeing me call her and deciding to send me to voice mail so she can keep talking to Delilah instead. She'll listen to the voice mail later, I tell myself. She'll hear about the wedding, and she'll call back.

She has to.

Linnea walks into her room, and I jump, as if she's caught me doing something wrong.

"You okay?" she asks.

I glance at my phone. I haven't even told her Saskia exists, because I'm too afraid she'll see right through me and know about my maybe crush. "I was just thinking about the plan," I say instead of the truth. "We have to sabotage the cake tasting next week."

"We could sprinkle salt over all the cakes," Linnea suggests, and I giggle.

"Or just pretend to hate them all. I bet the baker would get so mad he'd throw us out," I say.

"You're not a good enough actress for that," Linnea says.

I gasp, tossing my hand over my mouth. "How dare you!" I screech, pretending to get all offended, and we both burst into laughter.

"See?" she says, shaking her head. "You're a terrible actress. No one would ever buy you hating cake."

"Okay, well, what if I pretend to get sick?" I suggest.

Linnea's nose scrunches as she thinks. "That could work. For the venues, we just have to get everyone to say no to letting Dad and Sasha book them."

"If they can't find a place to have the wedding, they can't get married. You're a genius," I say. With plans this good, I feel ready to start preparing to leave for the city tonight. There's no way Mom and Harrison make it through a day of crumbling wedding plans without at least one major fight. I'll be packing my bags by this time tomorrow.

CHAPTER
ELEVEN

Mom hums as she drives, quieter than the radio but loud enough for me to hear. We're all packed into the car for a day of touring the venues, starting with a small botanical garden a few towns over.

"Can you imagine?" Mom says, meeting my eyes in the rearview mirror. "A ceremony in all those flowers?"

"I hope it's pretty," I tell her. Not that it matters— Linnea and I have developed a foolproof plan.

As soon as we park the car, I start putting said plan in action, lagging a bit behind the rest of the group as the owner, an older woman with gray curls and sparkling eyes, walks out of the reception office to welcome us.

"This space is so beautiful," Mom says, her eyes wide as she takes it in.

She's not wrong. Even though we're just standing in the driveway, the gentle smell of flowers drifts through the air, and the tree leaning over our car is thick with blossoms. Mom's right—it *would* be nice to have a wedding here. If it were anyone else getting married, I'd be all for it. But since it's Mom and Harristinks, the worst match ever, not even the sweetest-smelling rose could change my mind.

Instead, I slouch through the visit as the owner, Ms. Reilly, walks us down the cobblestone path winding through the gardens. I do my best to look worried, but I catch Linnea laughing at me a couple of times, so it's possible I look more like I'm pretending to be a bridge troll. Maybe she's right about my acting skills.

"And here's where you'd have the ceremony," Ms. Reilly says, stopping in front of a grassy stretch. Mom pauses, looking around and beaming.

"Perfect for a ceremony under the stars," Harrison says. "And lots of stargazing at the reception."

I roll my eyes. Of course he's bringing his telescope to the wedding. I hope the two of them will be very happy together.

"It's beautiful."

I hate to admit it twice in one day, even if I'm only

admitting it to myself, but she's right again. Ms. Reilly stopped under a yawning oak tree that shades a patch of grass where she's saying we can set up an awning for Mom and Harrison to stand under during the ceremony. At the bottom of the slope, there's a shimmery pond, huge lily pads floating on its surface.

It's pretty much a postcard for a perfect wedding venue.

"We'd love to look at your availability," Mom says, looping her arm through Harristinks' elbow.

"I'll get the paperwork," Ms. Reilly says with a smile.

Mom and Harrison walk ahead to the reception area, and I give Linnea a nod. She waits for George to catch up with them, falling into step beside me and Ms. Reilly.

"Are you excited for the wedding?" she asks us.

I take a deep breath. This is the part of the plan that's the scariest. I might get in trouble at school sometimes for talking to Saskia instead of taking notes, but I'm not one to be rude on purpose. But when it comes to the plan, I'll do anything. So I look her right in the eye and say, "No."

Ms. Reilly blinks at me, shock written all over her face. "Why on earth not?"

"The whole thing is just dumb." My sweat-slicked

palms are shaking in my pockets. I might not be as shy as Linnea, but this is pushing even my limits *way* past their comfort zone.

Next to me, Linnea looks ready to faint. I cross my fingers that she'll manage to choke out her lines. *Come on, Linnea,* I will her. *Be bold.*

"I wish . . ." Linnea takes a deep breath, swallowing. "I wish they weren't getting married at all."

Ms. Reilly purses her lips at us. "This doesn't seem like the kind of thing you should be going around telling people, and I'm not thrilled about the tone you've taken with me."

My face flushes as her eyes flash with anger. And then it gets a whole lot worse. Because I trip over a rock on the path and go flying into the flowerbed next to me. I don't stop there. No, I keep rolling down the little hill, crushing the tiny purple blooms under my flailing elbows.

"How dare you!" Ms. Reilly screeches from above me.

I sit up, wincing as I wipe pollen streaks from my face. My whole body feels like one giant bruise, but even that damage is nothing compared to what the flowers have suffered. The bed is ruined, petals crushed and stems ripped. Ms. Reilly's face is as purple as the battered flowers.

I get up slowly. I'm stuck right in the middle of the flowers, so I have no choice but to walk over them as I climb back up to the path.

Mom, Harristinks, and George come running up the path. Mom's face sinks when she sees Ms. Reilly's expression.

"I guess we'll . . . show ourselves out," she says quietly.

Ms. Reilly shoots me a look that makes my whole face flush. "I think that would be best."

And with that, she marches us back to the car.

Mom isn't humming as she drives away. "Well that was unfortunate."

"It was an accident, I swear," I say. It's not technically a lie—I didn't mean to fall and ruin all the flowers. The fact that it perfectly sabotaged the visit was just a bonus. A really bruise-covered bonus.

"I know," Mom says, meeting my eye in the rear-view mirror. "I can't believe how mad she was."

How rude we were before I fell probably had something to do with it, but I decide to keep that part to myself.

"Maybe the next one will be better," she says. "There's not much space for a reception there anyway. My hopes are higher for the restaurant."

"You can get married at a restaurant?" I ask skeptically.

"This one has a beautiful outdoor space where we could have a reception," Mom says. "And it would include catering, which makes our lives a little easier."

Not if I have anything to say about it.

The restaurant is a bit dark inside, and the outside space is too small. As we walk around the space, Mom's face looks like it does come report card day, when I hand her a string of Bs and Cs. I don't even need to sabotage this one; it's gone and sabotaged itself.

We pile back into the car for the third and final venue: the East Hammond library. It's a little building, but it has an event room lined with smooth wood shelves, the book bindings the only décor. It's a perfect space. It smells like old pages and wood finish, and I can almost see myself walking here after school and hanging out by the shelves.

"I sort of love it," Harrison says, his arm around Mom's waist.

"Even though you can't see the stars?" I mutter.

He hears me, but fortunately assumes I'm teasing him instead of being rude, and grins as he points out the window. "Don't worry, we'll have the reception outside. Tons of space for mapping."

When he says it, I feel bad. I don't like the telescope as much as he does—I don't think it's possible for anyone to like anything as much as Harrison loves his telescope—but he did go to all that trouble teaching me how to make star maps. Maybe I don't have to be quite so mean about it.

"Where can we talk about putting in a deposit?" Mom asks, turning to the librarian. She gestures to the front desk, and they make their way past me.

I crack my knuckles. Time to sabotage. Putting on my classic sad face, I sidle over to the librarian giving us the tour, and give a hefty sigh.

"What's wrong, honey?" she asks.

I glance over at Mom and Harrison, who are looking at the books on the other side of the room. "I don't know if I should say."

"I'm here if you want to talk," she says in that reassuring librarian tone.

"They're lying to you," I whisper. "They're pretending like they have this fairy-tale romance, but they only met three weeks ago."

The librarian's face falls, confusion wrinkling her brow. "What?"

"Never mind," I say quickly, and turn on my heel to walk away. Judging from her frown, which looks just like Ms. Reilly's purplish expression, we won't get this venue either, leaving us with no place to host the wedding.

I think I'll pack my books first.

I do my best to keep up the sad girl act, even though I feel like skipping as I cross the room back to Mom. Linnea joins us a minute later, a secret smile on her face. She must be as thrilled as I am that our plan is on the verge of succeeding.

But then the librarian crosses over to us. "Shall we look at available dates?"

She gives me a pointed look when Mom says yes, and I feel like shrinking under her sharp eyes. She must have seen right through me somehow. I'm not the best actress, after all.

"Yes," Mom says right away. "I'm absolutely in love with this place."

The librarian leads them to the front desk to look at the calendar, and Mom loops her arm around me as we follow her.

"What do you think?" she asks.

I glance around me. "It's pretty."

"I thought you might like the idea of a wedding surrounded by all these books," Mom says.

I glance up at her hopefully for a moment. Is she finally taking what I like into consideration? Because if so, boy do I have a list for her.

"You know what else I'd like?" I say, deciding to let her believe I'm in love with this wedding venue. It can only help my cause. "Visiting Saskia."

If I could just see her again, it could answer all my questions.

Mom looks down at me, her lips pursed. "Really, Autumn, I thought you were finally getting into the wedding planning. Why can't you step up and be part of this family?"

"I just—"

"Right now is about the wedding, okay?" Mom says, frowning at me. As if I didn't already know that. As if every conversation we've had the past month and a half hasn't been entirely about her stupid wedding. I get it: I don't matter at all.

She joins the librarian and Harristinks by the desk, leaving me to stare after them, yet another part of my plan completely ruined.

• • •

I never thought I'd be the one to say this, but, turns out, there *is* such a thing as too much cake. I plowed through the first slice, even though Mom told me to save room for all the wedding cakes we have to taste today, because who am I to turn down all that fancy icing?

Besides, my plan for cake tasting is to pretend to get sick. Shoving my face with cake will only make it more believable. After the complete failure I had with the venue visits, today's sabotage has to be a success.

The baker brings out a slice of the third cake right now, and it's frosted with swirling roses. Just looking at it, I can feel the excess frosting rising up my throat, bile burning my insides.

"Isn't this great?" Linnea asks. She has a smudge of the lemon icing from the last cake on the corner of her lips. I frown at her. This part of the plan relies on me, but she could help me out by at least pretending not to have the best day of her life.

"What do you rate that last one?" Harrison asks.

"Definitely a ten," George says, wiping his mouth with the back of his hand.

"You said that about the one before that, too," Linnea says in a teasing tone, the same one I always use when George starts bragging about how much taller he is than me. Hearing it from her mouth makes my stomach feel squirmy, like all that frosting is flip-flopping inside me.

"Well, it's all cake," George says, teasing her right back. "It all tastes amazing."

"This tastes like a garden," Linnea says after a bite.

Mom smiles at her so wide, I'm shocked her face

doesn't split in two. "What a lovely way to put it. I already loved the cake, but now I'm sold on it."

"Does that mean we're decided?" the baker asks.

"Oh, no, we're still very undecided," George says, shaking his head vigorously, his brown mop of hair rustling. "We should definitely keep tasting. Bring on more cake."

"A wise young man," he says, clapping George on the shoulder. "I always save the best for last."

He's not wrong. I wasn't sure how anything could top the sweet tartness of the lemon icing, but he brings out platefuls of what he calls champagne cake with lavender frosting. Even though my stomach is so full that I feel like the food is piling up my throat because it's run out of room, I take an eager bite. It's the best thing I've ever put in my mouth.

"This is so good," Linnea says. "But I really liked the garden."

Mom laughs. "So did I."

I swallow my mouthful, and it feels like sludge going down my throat. My stomach still swirls. Watching Mom listen to Linnea like she never seems to listen to me anymore, I'm starting to think I might not have to pretend to get sick at all.

"Are you a writer, Linnea?" Mom asks.

Linnea shakes her head, blushing.

"Don't be so modest," Harrison says. He licks the leftover lavender icing from his fork. "She won a prize last year. Best poem at the fifth-grade open mic night."

"That makes sense," Mom says. "You seem to have a real way with words."

Everyone keeps talking, not noticing that I'm getting sick for real. My stomach bubbles. I take a slow, deep breath, but the cake still feels like it's boiling inside me.

"Can I read the poem?" George asks.

I press the backs of my fingers against my mouth, struggling to swallow the saliva that's suddenly flooded against my tongue.

It's not enough.

"Where's your bathroom?" I ask through my hand, whirling around in my chair to face the baker.

He points to a little door behind the counter, and I spring from my chair, dashing across the linoleum floor. I rush as fast as I can, my stomach surging.

I don't make it in time.

Mom rushes over to me as soon as she finally notices that I'm sick. Not that it's possible to miss it now. The baker is super nice about the whole puking-all-over-his-store thing.

"It happens all the time," he says when Mom apologizes for me. "You're not the first to overdo it at a tasting."

"The cakes are just so good," Mom says with a smile.

My face flames red. "I'm sorry," I whisper.

"Don't you dare apologize," the baker tells me with a kind smile. "I'll get you a glass of water."

"You all right, honey?" Mom asks me.

I look up at her. I'm dying to tell her the truth. *No, I'm not all right,* I want to tell her. How can she not see that? How can she not know by now how bad I'm hurting?

I've tried telling her so many times this summer, but somehow, every time I try bringing it up, it turns into another conversation about *being part of the family* and *wedding planning takes priority right now.* If she doesn't understand by now, I don't know how to make her see. So instead, I just shrug.

"Guess the cake was just too rich for me," I say.

But at the end of the tasting, Mom still puts down a deposit to have the baker make her wedding cake.

CHAPTER TWELVE

Mom brings up the plans for her stupid wedding every ten seconds exactly. I know because I've started timing her at all our mealtimes. At dinner yesterday, she brought it up twenty-seven times, which beat the record set at the brunch we had a few days ago where she talked about floral arrangements alone for seven minutes straight. I've completely given up on trying to talk to her about Saskia, home, or anything that isn't related to white lace. I brought it up twice since the venue visit, and both times Mom shut me down to talk about what kind of fish she should serve. Overcooked salmon now ranks higher than my life falling to shambles around here.

We're having breakfast now, and I sit at the counter and eat my cereal and tick the seconds as they go by. Ten, nine, eight—

"Oh, honey," Mom says to Harrison. "Did I tell you I have a gown fitting scheduled for later this week? I can't believe how fast this is all moving."

"I'll make sure not to peek when you get back," Harrison says with a smile.

"You girls should come with me," Mom says, turning to me and Linnea. "It'll be so fun."

"And watch you try on wedding dresses?" Linnea's eyes are wide. "Can we help you pick?"

"Of course," Mom says. "Why else would I ask you to come? Now, tell me about tennis camp."

Linnea starts telling her about the progress I've made with my backhand in the past week, but I'm back to counting the seconds. Three, two, one—

"Oh, before I forget, where did you want your cousin in the seating chart?" Mom asks Harrison.

I bite my lip. If this wedding wasn't ruining my life, it would be sort of funny how much Mom can't stop talking about it. As it is, though, I really wish she'd be quiet.

"Put her as far away from my mom as possible," Harrison says with an eye roll.

"I have to run," Mom says. "I have a meeting with

the florist, and I'm booking a dance lesson for the girls on the way home. But we'll go over the details at dinner, all right?"

"Do you need help?" Linnea asks, straightening.

Mom beams at her. "I would love some help. Want to come?"

I watch them go, Linnea trotting after Mom—*my mom*—with her pale face all lit up at the thought of wedding flowers, and my eyes burn with tears. It's like Linnea fits better into my family than I do. Like she's stepped right into my place, leaving me on the outside looking in. Though I guess this gives her the chance to do some wedding planning sabotage of her own.

Mom glances over her shoulder at me when she reaches the doorway. An afterthought hovering on her lips. "Want to come, Autumn?"

I want to say yes. Not because I want to go help pick wedding flowers, but because I want to squeeze myself into their afternoon and force myself to fit.

My desire to stay as far away from the wedding planning wins out.

"No," I say, but as the front door shuts behind Mom and Linnea, I instantly regret it.

• • •

"Your mom is going to be the coolest stepmom ever," Linnea says.

I take a bite of my sandwich. It tastes like sawdust. I never thought I'd miss the days when George made my lunch because Mom was out of town visiting Harrison, but he has a way with food that no one else in the family—and by *family*, I mean me, Mom, and George—does.

We're sitting at our usual picnic table, tennis rackets leaning against the bench behind us.

"How was flower shopping?" I ask, trying my best to keep the sharp, jealous edge out of my voice. "Did you get any sabotage done?"

Mom came back looking happy, but maybe Linnea is playing a long game.

She grimaces. "I tried pretending to be allergic to all the flowers, but S-Mom saw right through me. She picked—"

"S-Mom?" I ask.

"Oh, yeah, we decided that's what I should call her," Linnea says, talking so fast it's a miracle her tongue doesn't trip over the words. "Her name is Sasha, and she's going to be my stepmom. It just works."

"But . . . she's . . ." She's *my* mom. I swallow. "Totally works."

"Don't know what you should call my dad," she adds. "H-Dad doesn't have the same ring to it."

"I'll probably stick to Harrist—Harrison," I say flatly. "My dad lives in California."

Not that I see Dad enough for him to belong in my little family. But still. I'm not about to replace him with Harristinks, some guy I barely know, just because Mom decided that he's her soul mate or whatever.

The smile drops off Linnea's face. She nods. "Yeah. Totally."

Dana jogs up the hill to us, clapping her hands on our shoulders when she reaches our table. "How are the two future stepsisters?"

She's beaming down at us. I look back up at her, and when she sees the look in my eyes, her eyebrows knit together for just a moment.

"We're great," Linnea says, but her voice sounds strained against her throat. For a moment, I feel bad. It's not her fault that my life is ruined.

Then again, she called my mom *S-Mom*. She's worming her way into my family, unaware that the closer she gets, the more she pushes me out. She's supposed to be helping me sabotage the wedding, not picking floral arrangements.

"We're starting back up in a few minutes, okay?"

151

Dana says, meeting my eye one last time before she jogs over to the next table.

I watch her go. This is Dana. The girl who kissed another girl in the parking lot. The girl who saw the look in my eyes.

I can't talk to Mom, or George, or Linnea about Saskia. None of them will listen. None of them would get it. They all have the kinds of crushes people expect them to have. Mom with Harristinks, Linnea and whatever boy she wouldn't tell her friends about. If I told them I miss Saskia, they would just think I miss her as a friend. And I don't know if I miss her as a friend or as something else. As a *crush*. None of them would understand.

But maybe Dana would.

• • •

Wedding dress shopping might just turn out like the restaurant: ready to sabotage itself. At least, that's how it seems as Linnea and I parse through racks and racks of white dresses at the boutique Mom took us to. Every dress is a lace monstrosity that's going to make Mom look more like the abominable snowman than a bride.

"This one's sort of cute," Linnea says, her voice meek as the store owner walks past us. She's a middle-aged woman who tried to make small talk with us when we walked in, and Linnea clammed up as soon as this new adult tried to talk to her. Still now, her face is paler than usual, and she sounds like she's a million miles away even though she's standing right next to me. I stare at her. This girl needs some serious coming out of her shell.

I wait until the store owner has drifted over to where Mom is standing by the fitting rooms, well out of earshot, before I shake my head at her. "No, it isn't."

Linnea blushes, her cheeks splotching as she glances over her shoulder to make sure the store owner is out of earshot. "I mean, yeah, but . . ."

Grinning, I pull a particularly ugly dress off the rack—one with puffy sleeves and a massive trailing bow on the butt—and hold it out in front of me.

"Should we show her this one?"

Linnea bites her lip to keep from laughing. "Put it back!"

"Or this one?" I ask, swapping Bow Disaster Dress for one that is inexplicably fluffy. This time, Linnea can't keep her giggles inside.

"Look at this one," Linnea whispers. The pink recedes from her cheeks as she pulls a hanger off the rack.

I dissolve into giggles. The dress she found is a cupcake monstrosity, with huge puffs everywhere and lace dripping from every stitch of fabric. If Mom put it on, she'd look like a snow beast.

"Bet I can beat it," I say, turning back to the racks and flipping through the gowns until I reach one that's baggy around the waist and thighs, but cinched around the knees. Linnea just stares at it, her mouth gaping.

"How is that even supposed to work?" she says, tilting her head as she examines it.

I laugh at her expression. "I think we can agree that I found the ugliest dress in the store."

"Not so fast." Linnea, forgetting her earlier discomfort entirely, ducks under the rack she's been examining to get to the back of the store. I follow her, ready to continue bragging about my certain victory, but she turns to me triumphantly, holding a gown that has what can only be described as white lace polka dots detailing its sheer sides.

I give her a round of applause. "Okay, okay. You've bested me at my own game."

Linnea takes an elaborate bow. "Let's get S-Mom to try it on."

"That's a great idea." I beam, trying to push past the sticky feeling I get in my throat when Linnea calls my mom *S-Mom*. "If she thinks this store only has ugly dresses, she'll give up."

"Perfect sabotage," Linnea agrees, offering her hand for a high five.

I follow Linnea to the front of the store, where Mom is contemplating a too-frilly dress.

"S-Mom?" she says, holding out the dress. "I think we found the one."

Mom turns to us eagerly, and bites her lip when she sees the dress we've picked out. "Oh my God. Girls. Be nice, the owner is around here somewhere."

But even though she's got her best be-reasonable-Autumn tone on, I can tell she's trying not to laugh.

"Just try it on," I say through a giggle, as if this is all one big joke, and not my best attempt at sabotaging the dress hunt.

Seeing our smiles, Mom gives in and takes the dress from Linnea's hands. "All right, I'll add it to my stack."

She disappears into the dressing room, leaving Linnea and me to mill around in the front of the store until she emerges, clad in polka-dot lace and looking absolutely ridiculous.

"What do you think?" she asks, twirling.

I clap my hand over my mouth, and Linnea has to stuff her knuckles into her mouth so that her laugh doesn't attract the attention of the lady working in the boutique today, who's busy helping another bride parse through veils.

"I think it's the one," Linnea says when she's recovered from her giggle fit.

"Definitely buy it," I agree.

Mom shakes her head at us. "You two are too much."

The next hour is a parade of bad dresses. Most of them looked like they'd be good on the rack, but then Mom slips into them and finds something wrong with them. The lace is too itchy. The fabric bunches too much at her hips. The train is too dramatic.

The list of flaws goes on and on, and every time Mom comes out of the dressing room draped in another failure, she looks a little more dejected. Maybe she's realizing that, like these dresses, the whole wedding looked good on the rack, but now that she's trying it on, it's full of mistakes.

A girl can dream, right?

I'm about to suggest that we give up and go get dinner when Mom comes back out in her latest find. Right away, I can tell something's different. She's standing up straighter as she walks into the room. The dress is just long enough that it makes her look like she's floating as she steps toward us, and her smile lights up her face.

Next to me, Linnea actually gasps when she sees it.

"It's perfect," she whispers.

I swallow. It is.

"I love it," Mom says with a smile.

My thoughts are rushing a mile a minute. I thought the place had sabotaged itself. How can I stop this from happening? Maybe I can change the price tag to make it look out of budget, or dot a stain onto the back to convince her not to buy it, or—

"This is the one," the boutique lady says, rushing over to Mom, and before I can put any of my plans into action, Mom swaps her credit card for a dress, and another part of my plan is ruined, another day bringing us closer to the wedding.

CHAPTER
THIRTEEN

Instead of bouncing straight to the kitchen the way the smell of bacon makes me want to, I tiptoe down the hall, sneaking past the door. Mom keeps the wedding seating chart in Harrison's office, and I have one last sabotage plan idea left.

Mom wants a small wedding, so there are only a few tables to work with. But I make quick work: putting Aunt Hailey next to Mom's cousin, since they hate each other, and kicking Grandma out of the family table and into a random side table full of Mom's college friends she doesn't even like that much. I grab a few other names at random and switch them around. By the time I'm done, it's a hot mess.

And with that, I skip over to the kitchen. Mom will see it, and she'll be annoyed that Harrison messed with her work. A fight is sure to follow.

My stomach tightens as I sit. The cake episode from two days ago still haunts me, so I push my eggs around my plate without daring to actually eat them. Linnea comes in a few minutes after me.

"Are you excited for the dance lesson?" she asks me.

I stare at her blankly. "Dance lesson?"

"Yeah," Linnea says cheerily—way too cheerily for a conversation about dance lessons this early in the morning—as she pours herself a glass of orange juice. "Remember? S-Mom said she was going to get them for us. For the wedding?"

None of this is ringing a bell, but it feels like the kind of thing that might as well happen. I'm already stuck in East Hammond, stuck with a best friend I may or may not have a crush on but who definitely won't text me back, and stuck in the middle of this wedding planning. Might as well throw in dance lessons, too.

"And Katie and Erica are coming," Linnea adds, because of course they are.

Wait a second.

"Are they invited to the wedding?" I ask.

Linnea nods. "Their moms are teachers at the school, too, so Dad is friends with them."

I close my eyes and take a deep breath. So I'm not even allowed to *see* Saskia, but Linnea gets to bring her pals to the wedding? I know Mom was too busy single-mom-ing to become super-close friends with Saskia's mom, but doesn't the fact that *I'm* super-close friends with Saskia count for anything at all?

"I think it'll be fun," Linnea says in a small voice that makes me feel bad. It's not her fault that dating Harristinks has transformed Mom from the coolest parent ever to basically Cinderella's stepmom.

"Super fun," I tell her, even though I'm grinding my teeth. I remind myself about the seating chart sabotage and return to my breakfast. At least there's still a chance this plan could work.

But then Mom walks into the room, and she has this smile on her face that's unlike any other smile I've ever seen on her. It makes my stomach twist again. She's . . . glowing. That's the word they use in all the rom-coms when they talk about brides-to-be. *Glowing.* Has she not seen the seating chart mess yet?

Thinking of my mom as a bride is even worse than thinking about her having a boyfriend, and I can't be in this room with her and all her wedding glow right now. So I force a smile on my face.

"When are the dance lessons?" I ask.

"In about an hour, so finish up quick," Mom tells me.

As soon as I declare myself done with breakfast, I creep back into the office. The seating chart is back to normal. It's as if I was never in here at all. Did Mom see it and fix it without saying anything?

Frowning, I slump back to my room to get dressed.

Half an hour later, I'm buckled into the back seat of Harrison's car, trying not to think about how Saskia and I were supposed to be taking the subways by ourselves all summer. Instead, I have to be chaperoned around, strapped in a car I can't drive without an adult.

"It's nice you're spending more time with Linnea's friends," Harrison says as we turn onto the highway. "It'll be great for you to start at a new school with some friends already."

I nod, but his words only remind me why my plan—the plan that's currently falling apart around me—is so important. I don't want to start at East Hammond Middle School in the fall, no matter how many new friends I manage to make before the year starts. The one friend that counts won't be there, and that's all I need to know.

Harrison drops us off in front of a small white-painted building, and leads us inside. Katie and Erica are already waiting by the reception office. They hug me like we go back way further than one awkward picnic.

"I heard you're going to be in school with us next

year," Katie says brightly. I grit my teeth as I nod in response.

"Maybe you'll find someone you like," Erica adds, "now that there are more than eleven boys in your grade. Since you won't tell us who your New York crush is."

"The secretive sisters," Katie says, giggling. "We'll get your crushes out of you one way or another."

Her tone is a friendly teasing, but next to me, Linnea turns a deep red, clearly embarrassed by her words. Still, she laughs along with them. So much for taking my advice and being bold.

"All right, girls, I'll pick you up in two hours," Harristinks says after he finishes checking us in with the receptionist.

I stare after him longingly. *Two hours?* What could we possibly have to learn that requires that much time?

As it turns out—a lot.

A woman in a flashy orange top waltzes out of the main office, clapping her hands together when she sees us.

"Are you Ms. Sinclair's girls?" she asks us, rubbing her hands together as she stops in front of us.

"Yes," Linnea and I say at the same time.

I shoot her a look out of the corner of my eye. "I am."

"I'm Miss Angela," she says. "Are we excited for the wedding?"

I join Linnea, Katie, and Erica in nodding. I doubt confessing my true feelings to Miss Angela and her very bright shirt will do anything to help my cause.

"Well, your mom"—Miss Angela glances at me for a moment, then looks back to Linnea—"and stepmom wants you all to learn a bit of waltz so that you can rock it on that wedding dance floor."

She puts her hands up in loose fists in front of her and does a little shake. Her excitement is almost infectious, and by the time we're following her into the studio, I'm hoping this won't be the two hours of torture I assumed it would be.

Then Miss Angela shows us the first steps she wants us to practice.

"So it's just counting the music to guide you through these steps," she says, moving smoothly around the room. She adds a twirl, and I jump out of her way.

Yeah, there's no way I can do that.

She starts the music, and I do my best to keep up with Katie, who falls in line with the notes as if the music's coming from her bones. Meanwhile, Linnea and I shuffle behind her as if we never learned to count to four.

I make eye contact with her in the mirror lining one side of the studio, and as soon as she spots the frazzled look on my face, she bites her lip like she's stifling laughter. The music keeps going, so I try a twirl like Miss Angela did. I must've pulled it off wrong, though, because I end up crashing straight into Linnea.

She trips over my feet, her elbows digging into my rib cage as we tumble on top of each other on the floor. I'm laughing before I'm done falling, and I can feel Linnea giggling too.

"Are you all right?" Miss Angela asks.

We both nod as we clamber to our feet.

"Well, I see why we needed the practice," she says with a grin. "Let's try it again from the beginning."

We spend the next hour "trying again from the beginning," and it becomes clear that Miss Angela's favorite word is *again*, said with a flourish and a smile. My legs feel like jelly beneath me, and by the time she says we can have a water break, it's a miracle I can stand, let alone wobble my way to where my water bottle is sitting with the rest of my stuff by the water fountain just outside the studio.

Sweat dripping from every surface of my skin, I land hard on the floor and take a long drink from my water bottle. As we drink, Linnea and her friends talk about who they want to be on their teams next year.

"What sport do you guys play?" I ask between sips.

Erica laughs. "What? I mean, I play softball, and Linnea does tennis."

"I don't do sports," Katie says, tossing her hair. "I want to be a ballerina."

"Oh, then what teams—" I start.

Erica cuts me off with another laugh. "That's for our classes. They split each grade up into teams, and then each team has the same teacher for every subject."

I blink. "Why can't we just all have the same teachers?"

At my school in the city, we had one teacher per subject in each grade. Next year, I was supposed to have Ms. Stevenson for English, like all the other seventh graders.

"The grades are too big," Linnea explains. "So we're split up into groups of four. I hope we get the same team."

"Same," I murmur. I can't imagine going to a school with that many people in it.

It feels funny, thinking of something in East Hammond as bigger than my home in New York City, which has millions more people. But even though the city was bigger, I divided it up into small bits. My little family, which was just Mom and George and me. My small school, with my even smaller homeroom class.

My friendship with Saskia, just the two of us. The city might be big, but when I lived there, I knew exactly where I belonged.

East Hammond is tiny, but I don't belong anywhere here. Not with my family anymore, now that Mom is all in love with Harrison and too busy planning her wedding to notice that I hate it here, and George ready to go to college in just a few weeks. Not with Saskia, who's already replaced me with some random new friend. Definitely not with Linnea's friends and their terrifying questions about crushes.

East Hammond might as well be the ocean—so big I'm always lost, so deep I have to kick all my muscles all the time just to keep from drowning.

"I have to go to the bathroom," I say. "Do you know where it is?"

I don't really have to pee, but I do need a break from talking about how huge their school is, so I scramble out of the room when Miss Angela points me in the right direction. I shut the rickety door behind me and sit on the toilet, taking deep breaths until the awful tightening swirly feeling in my stomach eases a bit. When my insides calm, I get up and force myself back to the dance studio.

I see Linnea and her friends huddled around the water fountain before they see me, and I get close enough that I can hear their conversation. I'm about to wave when Linnea's words force me to stop in my tracks.

"I've always wanted a sister," she's saying. "I'm so excited for the wedding."

I freeze midstep. She's always wanted a sister?

She's supposed to be on my side. She's supposed to agree with me. She's supposed to be helping me. But my plan is falling apart, and I just found out my escape partner is *excited for the wedding.*

I clear my throat loudly as I walk up, and Linnea jumps when she sees me. I lead them back into the studio, pretending I didn't hear a single word she said, but her words keep thrumming through my head.

"Are we ready to get going again?" Miss Angela asks, and we all nod.

I follow the girls as we go back to our awkward waltzing, but I'm so wrapped up in my own thoughts that I can barely even pretend to listen to them for the rest of our time pas de bourrée-ing around the smooth marley floors of the studio. Linnea's voice is ringing too loud in my ears.

I've always wanted a sister.

If she already sees me as a sister, what does that mean for my escape?

•••

Linnea collapses onto her bed, her legs flattening against the mattress as she groans in relief. My muscles are aching, but I'm too full of nervous energy to copy her. She's *excited* for the wedding, and I can't get the thought out of my head.

I clear my throat, and she spins to face me.

"I heard you telling Katie and Erica that you've always wanted a sister," I say. Her smile slips off her face as I keep going. "That you're excited for the wedding?"

"I was just—" Linnea's face turns bright red, and I know right away that whatever she's about to say next isn't true.

"And everything with my plan has been going wrong," I say, folding my arms. "Are you actually on my side?"

Linnea looks down at her feet. "I didn't want to tattle. I thought maybe while you were trying to escape, I could convince you to stay."

"What do you mean?" I ask, my voice shaking.

"I thought maybe if we worked together and got to know each other better, you'd see that we could make pretty good stepsisters. And then maybe you'd want to stay," she says quietly.

I stare at her. "So this whole time, you've been sabotaging my sabotage. Oh my God." I blink with realization. "You put the seating chart back this morning. You told the librarian that I lied to her so she'd let them book the venue."

She nods without looking at me. "And I came up with the picnic to make sure we'd still have a good time after you ruined Dad's dinner. I made sure Dad saw how well S-Mom handled the emergency we used to ruin their date night. I lied about pretending to be allergic to the flowers, and I was secretly looking for good dresses for your mom while you picked all those bad ones."

"How could you?"

She was my only ally. It was just her and Saskia, but she's been ruining my plans since the beginning, and Saskia has already replaced me. Plus, Erica's crush questionnaire has left me terrified every time I talk to Saskia. I haven't called her in ages because I'm afraid of what my feelings will tell me when I hear her voice.

And now *this*?

"They end up a happy family at the end of the movie," Linnea says quietly. She sounds like she's about to cry, but I'm too mad to care. "I thought maybe that could happen with us. If I showed you the beach and we had fun times as a family, like on the picnic. I thought maybe it'd change things for you, and then we could be real sisters. It'd be like a lifelong slumber party."

"So you betrayed me for a slumber party?"

"The slumber party isn't the point," she says, rolling her eyes. "I wanted us to get along. To be like actual sisters who do stuff together and love to spend time together. It's not like you've been super nice to me, either," Linnea says, her voice suddenly forceful. "You didn't even give me a *chance* before you decided I wasn't good enough to be part of your family."

I stare at her. When I told her to be bold, this was *so* not what I had in mind.

"If you just give it a chance, it could be good," Linnea says, meeting my eye.

"Well it won't," I say, and I spin on my heel, ready to storm to the kitchen.

I have to save the plan somehow, but I have no idea how. What can I try that Linnea hasn't already ruined?

When I round the corner, I see Mom and Harristinks locked up in a hug. Mom's cheek rests against Harrison's chest, her eyes closed and a little smile on her face. Harrison's chin is on the top of her head. Their arms are wrapped tight around each other. They look so . . . in love.

I back out of the room, sliding my feet against the tiled floor as quietly as I can. This moment isn't something I want to walk into. I cough loudly as I round the corner again so that they know I'm coming this time. Mom still has the little smile on her face when she sees me, and I realize with a dreadful heaviness that I haven't seen her this happy in a long time. Maybe ever.

Looking at them, the way they smile at each other and touch hands as they cook dinner, I realize that my plan was super stupid. There's no way Mom and Harrison are going to break up, no matter how much Linnea ruined my sabotage plans. They must be something like soul mates. Mom's found where she belongs, and it's right here. In East Hammond, far away from my home in the city.

But where does that leave me?

CHAPTER
FOURTEEN

I pace around Linnea's bedroom, staring at the carpet. Thanks to Linnea, my plan is completely ruined. Worse than that, I'm not even sure it could have ever worked. I saw it yesterday when I walked in on Mom and Harrison all gooey-eyed and happy together.

But I still don't want to be stuck here.

I can't stand the thought of Linnea's room becoming *our* room, a place we share as sisters. Mom and Harrison might be in love, but that doesn't mean I want to be in the same family as her. Not after the way she backstabbed me.

That's when I spot my map of East Hammond on the shared desk. The one I labeled with all the places

Linnea showed me: the beach, the summer fair, the house we've lived in together. All the places where I *thought* we were planning together, conspiring to make sure I could get back home.

I cross over to the desk and cross them all out. It was all a pack of lies anyway. When I'm done, there's no space left for me here, nothing for me to label. No places or people in East Hammond I can call my own. How can a place like this be my home?

"Autumn," Mom calls from down the hall. "Dinner's ready."

"My stomach hurts again," I call back.

"Come anyway, I'll make you some ginger tea," Mom says.

Sighing, I tear myself away from the world's saddest map and go to the kitchen. Everyone else is already gathered around the kitchen island. They look just fine without me, one cozy little Autumn-less family.

I slide into my seat, glaring at my plate. This is supposed to be my family, but everyone around me has done nothing but let me down all summer. Mom has completely ignored how miserable I am, George is getting ready to abandon me any second, and Linnea has been actively sabotaging me this whole time. It's Harrison's fault I'm stuck here in the first place. How are any of them supposed to be my family?

"I made you some tea," Mom says, sliding a mug across the island. "It'll help your stomach."

I take a sip. It's sharp and bitter, burning my tongue. I make a face as it boils down my throat.

"Oh, it's not that bad," Mom says. "Finish it up."

I set the mug back on the counter. "I don't want to."

"It's good for you," Mom says.

"I said, I don't want to," I snap.

Mom frowns, putting her hands on her hips. "Autumn, what's wrong with you?"

"What's wrong with *me*?" I say. I can hear my voice climbing higher than I mean it to, until I'm shouting, but I don't care. It's like everything I felt at the cake-tasting place, the way I've felt all summer since we got here, has finally started bubbling up, like water when it starts to boil. Huge festers that pop and explode, anger spilling out of my mouth until it's too late to stop it.

I jump out of my chair. "What's wrong with *me*? Everything is wrong with me. I've been trying to tell you, and you just won't listen. What's wrong with me is that I hate it here, and I hate this pretend family, and I miss my apartment and my friends and I want to go *home*."

"What's going on?" Harrison asks. Linnea stares at me with a look of shock on her face. Like she can't imagine I'm still upset about moving to her perfect little town.

"Nothing," I say, backing away from them. "Don't mind me. I'd hate to ruin your perfect new lives having a perfect new family."

I take another step backward, and it's a step too far. The backs of my legs collide with something solid, and there's a giant crash. I whirl around in time to see Harrison's telescope hit the floor.

It's a disaster. The tripod is bent out of shape. The glass on both sides is broken, shattered into little bits across the floor. The long telescope itself is twisted into two parts.

My heart hammers in my throat as I spin back around to face Mom, Harrison, George, and Linnea. Mom's hands are clapped around her mouth. Harrison's face is drawn in horror. Linnea just stares at me, the same way she was before the telescope was broken. That's how I know I've gone too far.

"I didn't mean—" I don't know how to continue. I'm still too mad, and even though I didn't break the telescope on purpose, they'll blame me for it like I meant to do it all along. And there are tears burning in my throat.

Instead of finishing my sentence, I run all the way to Linnea's room and hide under my blankets.

CHAPTER
FIFTEEN

Everyone is silent at breakfast. The awful sound of chewing fills the kitchen, interrupted only by the sound of someone's fork scraping against their plate as we stab bites of Harrison's French toast into our mouths.

I know it's my fault. The broken telescope has been cleared away, all the bits of glass swept into the garbage, but it might as well still be there, haunting me with its destroyed frame.

Linnea gets up to put her plate in the dishwasher first, filing silently out of the kitchen. Mom is next, then George, leaving just me to finish eating across from Harrison.

I put my fork down before my last bite and look up at him. I have to take a deep breath before I can get the words out. "I'm sorry."

Harrison nods. "Thank you for saying that."

He doesn't seem like he forgives me, but I don't know what else to say. I pick up my fork and take my last bite. I haven't done enough, but what else can I do?

"I know you didn't mean it, Autumn, but you hurt everyone's feelings last night," Harrison says. "I know you're sorry, but I hope you can find a way to make it right."

I nod. I'm not quite sure what he means, and the awkwardness of the moment is making me uncomfortable, so I shuffle out of the room, passing Mom on my way out.

She gives me a once-over, her eyes tight. "What's going on, Autumn?"

I look up at her, hope surging in my chest. Did she just . . . ask about me? Not the wedding?

I rack my brains, trying to figure out where to start. *What's going on* is sort of a complicated question to ask me these days. But before I can so much as open my mouth to tell her how much I hate everything right now, she sighs.

"This behavior is just unacceptable," she says. "The

wedding is a week away, and you've still made no effort to join in."

She may as well have crumpled up my heart like it's last week's homework. All the words I'd been about to let spill out of me die in my throat, and I don't say anything at all in response.

Shaking her head, she walks past me into the kitchen. I linger in the doorway, crossing my fingers. She seems annoyed, and Harrison is certainly angry enough. Maybe this is the big fight I've been waiting for.

"I'm so worried about Autumn," Mom says quietly.

I slump against the wall. Or maybe not.

"She's adjusting," Harrison says. "It's normal."

"It's not like her to act like this," Mom says. Her tone is so disappointed, it makes me want to shrink until I'm small enough to hide in the cracks between the floorboards.

I've ruined everything, and I have no idea how to fix it. Worse still—thanks to the broken telescope, absolutely no one actually heard what I was trying to say.

● ● ●

The last few serves of the day feel like they take forever. I miss every ball Alice, my partner for the afternoon, hits at me. I can't help it. My mind is scattered in a million different directions, all paths leading back to Dana.

She finally blows her whistle for the end of the day, and I drop my racket. Before Linnea can reach me and tell me about how *S-Mom* is waiting for us in the parking lot, I run over to Dana.

"Can I talk to you?" I ask her quickly.

She raises an eyebrow, nodding. "Of course."

She leads me to a shady patch of grass between the tennis courts and the picnic table, tipping her head to one side. "There's a lot changing for you right now, isn't there?"

"You don't know the half of it," I tell her. Then I think of the blond girl in the parking lot. "Actually. You might. That's why I wanted to ask you."

Dana's eyebrows shoot up. "Me? I've gotta be honest, I've lived in East Hammond my whole life. I've never moved anywhere. I mean, I can imagine what it's like, but—"

"Is the blonde your girlfriend?" I ask, rushing the words so much before I lose my nerve that they sound like one giant smooshed-together word. *Istheblondeyourgirlfriend?*

She blinks at me, a tiny smile peeking onto the corners of her lips. "Oh. Oh. Yes, she is. I'm a lesbian, and Lucy is my girlfriend."

My eyes fill with tears. They surprise me, and one trips down my cheek before I can stop it. I dab it away with a fingertip, blinking the rest back before they can overwhelm me.

"Oh, hon," Dana whispers, crouching to meet my eyes. "Hey, it's okay. You're okay."

I shake my head. "I'm not. I'm really not. I thought she was my best friend. I mean, she's my favorite person to spend time with, and the only one who gets all my jokes, and she has the best laugh in the whole world. She's in all my favorite memories. But then Erica said all this stuff about crushes, and now I think maybe I have a crush on her, and I don't know what I'm supposed to do about it or how I'm supposed to know the difference."

"Can I give you a hug?" Dana whispers.

I open my mouth to answer, and realize for the first time that I'm crying in earnest now. The tears drip from my eyelashes and the tip of my nose. I'm a hot, sniffling mess.

I nod instead, and Dana wraps her arms around my shoulders. "It's going to be okay," she whispers. "Want to tell me about it?"

She pulls back, meeting my red-rimmed eyes, and I nod.

"Her name is Saskia," I say, very quietly, terrified

anyone else will overhear. "We've been best friends since forever. And I never had a crush on anyone, but Mom always said I'd find the right boy one day. And then one of Linnea's friends told me what it really feels like to have a crush. And now I think I have a crush on her. How am I supposed to know for sure?"

Dana squeezes my shoulder. "I think that's a question only you can answer. But I can tell you this. Most girls who don't have crushes on girls also don't spend a lot of time worrying about whether or not they might have a crush on a girl."

"What do you mean?" I ask.

"Just that sometimes the fact that you think you might have a crush on her is enough," she says. "If you had a crush on a boy, no one would ask you to prove it. You could just . . . have a crush. It's the same thing when you have a crush on a girl. But you're so young and these are such hard questions for you to answer. You have time to find the answers that are right for you."

I stare up at her. Maybe she's right. If I didn't have a crush on Saskia, I wouldn't have thought of her in the first place when Erica asked me all those questions. I would think about her the way I think about all my other friends. The place she has in my heart is different, special. It always has been. This is just the first time I've had a name to put on that place. That special Saskia-sized room in my heart.

"I think I have a crush on her," I whisper. As soon as I say the words out loud, as soon as I admit them to myself, it feels like a huge weight rolls off my shoulders, and I can breathe again. I may not know where I fit in with my family, but I finally know where I fit in with myself.

"Then my advice?" Dana says with a little smile. "Don't let her get away."

"She's already gotten away," I point out. "Or, well, I'm the one who's moved away."

She's already found a new friend, moved on.

"Well, what does your mom think about you visiting her?"

I shrug. "Wedding planning is keeping her busy."

"Talk to her about it," Dana says softly. "I'm sure she'd understand better if she knew how you were feeling."

Talk to her about it. As if that's not what I've been trying to do this entire time. Before I can say anything, Linnea runs up to us, and I quickly dry my face before she reaches us and sees I've been crying.

"Hey, I was looking for you," she says. "S-Mom is here."

I nod. "Okay. I . . . um . . . thank you," I add, looking

back at Dana before following Linnea out to the parking lot.

I want to take Dana's advice. If I could just get Mom to understand, it could fix everything. But she won't listen to me. She's been refusing to listen all summer long. And now that everyone blames me for breaking Harrison's telescope, she's only going to want to listen less.

●●●

As soon as I get home from camp, I head straight for Harrstinks' pantry, rummaging through the sacks of sugar and canned goods until I find a box of hot chocolate mix. Saskia and I have always thought that hot chocolate should be a year-round beverage. Mom and George disagree—they're firm "hot chocolate is for the winter" kind of people—but I think the warmth and chocolatey smell are comforting even on the sweatiest of summer days.

Gripping a packet tight in one hand, I shuffle into the kitchen, switching on the electric kettle and dumping the powder into an empty mug. I hop onto the counter next to the kettle, letting my legs swing against the bottom cabinets as I wait for it to whistle. As soon as it does, I splash the water over the powder and swirl the mug to dissolve all the bits.

Footsteps patter down the hall, and I throw myself back off the counter, the soles of my feet stinging a bit as they hit the tile floor hard. Whoever is about to walk into the room is mad at me, and I'm not in the mood to be yelled at some more. Instead, I snatch my hot chocolate and round the corner into the living room just before they slip in.

It's Harristinks. I recognize his voice, and I'm instantly glad I got out of the kitchen in time. I can't handle another lecture from him about how my apologies aren't good enough.

"I know," he's saying. "I don't know how to fix it."

He pauses for a while, but I can't hear anyone answer. He must be on the phone.

"Yeah, she really did a number on it," he says with a low chuckle. "Every lens is shattered. No way we can stargaze at the wedding, I guess."

My stomach sinks. He's talking about *me*. Guess there's no hiding from this lecture after all. Still, I can't get myself to run away into the living room. It should be easy to just leave, but I'm too curious about what he'll say next.

"I know, I can't believe we have to get rid of her," he says.

My jaw drops. *Get rid of her?* I break one stupid telescope and I'm to be *gotten rid of*?

There's no way. Mom isn't going to let him.

He pauses a moment, listening to whatever monster is on the other end of the line, and then laughs. "Yeah, you're right. That does make me feel better."

The thought of getting rid of me makes him feel better. My whole body's shaking as I stand, leaving my mug of hot chocolate on the floor, and step back around the wall, into the kitchen.

Harristinks looks up at me, giving me a small smile. As if he hasn't just been talking about getting rid of me a mere moment ago.

"Hey, want any particular snacks?" he says, gesturing to the phone. "Your mom is just at the grocery store."

If I thought I was shocked before, it's nothing compared to the way I'm feeling now. My heart might as well be playing hopscotch with my stomach given how jumbled and jumping my insides feel.

Harristinks is on the phone *with Mom*?

Given how loudly he laughed at her response, she must have agreed to get rid of me. Harristinks finally asked her to choose between him and me, and she chose him. They'll be shipping me off to boarding school the moment they say *I do*.

"No," I say. It's a miracle I manage to choke a single word out.

My throat is tight with the threat of more tears, but I won't give Harristinks the satisfaction of seeing them. Instead, I shove past him and wait until I'm out of his line of sight before I make a mad dash for Linnea's bedroom, where I barricade myself in bed.

CHAPTER
SIXTEEN

I was up half the night trying to think of a new plan. Something so big, so explosive, that it would ruin the wedding once and for all. I've tried everything—chipping away at Mom and Harrison's relationship, sabotaging their wedding, talking to Mom like Dana said I should—and none of it has worked.

Worse, all of it has blown up in my face every time. Still, now that Harristinks has convinced Mom to *get rid* of me, I have no choice but to make it work.

Somewhere between two a.m. and my second sneak trip to the kitchen for late-night snacks, I came up with the perfect plan. Something that will stop the wedding flat and make Harristinks look so bad, Mom won't be able to laugh it off.

I just need to get up before anyone else. So when the alarm I set on my phone beeps at six in the morning, I pounce on it despite the bone-deep grogginess dragging my body down and switch it off before Linnea wakes up too. I wait in the early morning stillness, barely daring to breathe. Linnea shifts in her sheets, so I count my breaths for a minute, waiting, my heart hammering so hard I'm afraid the sound of it will wake her.

When a few minutes have passed and Linnea hasn't moved again, I slip out of bed and make my way to the door as quietly as I can. The bedroom door creaks treacherously when I open it, and I freeze in the doorway. This time, Linnea doesn't so much as roll over, so I wait a few seconds before tiptoeing down the hall to Harrison's office.

Mom and Harristinks decided to write their own vows. Harrison is all proud of his—he got them printed on fancy cardstock paper after he finished writing them, so he can read them at the wedding.

Without his cards, he won't remember his vows, and without his vows, he can't possibly marry my mom.

Now I just have to find where he put it.

I start my hunt on his desk, which is distressingly messy. I shift through the stacks of papers, trying not to move them too much so he doesn't notice I was here. I stumble across our first draft of our star map, and my heart tugs at me for a moment. *Maybe I shouldn't be doing this,* it seems to say with each beat. He makes Mom happy. Maybe she deserves to hear those vows he wrote for her.

But then I remember the way his face changed when I walked back into his telescope. The way Mom yelled at me instead of listening. The way Linnea betrayed me, the way George already has one foot out the door so far he doesn't seem to care about me at all anymore.

I drop the star map back on his desk and slide open the first desk drawer. It's full of stray school supplies— pencils, a broken crayon, three rulers, a notebook with a torn-up cover—but no cardstock vows. I'm about to open the next one when the office door swings open.

I'm so startled, I jump about a mile high. My heart is in my throat when I look up to see Linnea standing in the doorway, her arms folded across her chest.

My throat is so tight I can barely swallow as she takes a step into the room, frowning.

"What are you looking for?"

"Just . . . um . . ." I look around the desk. "Why are you awake?"

"I heard your alarm," Linnea says. "You're a way

deeper sleeper than you think you are. It'd been going off for like, five full minutes."

Heat creeps across my face. So much for my sneak attack.

"Why do you hate it here so much?" she asks softly. "I thought you were starting to like it. I thought we had a shot at being a family."

I look down at my bare feet, trying not to think about the summer fair, or the secret spots Linnea took me to at the beach, or any of the tiny adventures we could have planned.

"You know I've wanted a sister my whole life. And now it's like you're leaving me behind," she says, and I can hear the tears welling in her eyes without having to look up at her.

I meet her eyes, and a wave of guilt crashes over me. She wants the same thing I do: her family and her home. We just have different definitions of what those things look like. It's not her fault that what we both want pitted us against each other from the start.

"This isn't about East Hammond, or you," I tell her. "It's just something I have to do."

She must hear the tears building in my voice, too, because instead of arguing, she crosses the office and pulls open a thin drawer under Harrison's desk that I hadn't even noticed.

"This what you're looking for?" she says, giving me a small smile.

Harrison's vows are inside, and I find myself staring back at her, this girl who I just met, who would be my sister by this time next week. The girl who caught me about to shred our parents' marriage, and understood—like no one else did—that I *need* to go.

The tears threaten me again. I pull her into a hug. She gives a tiny huff of surprise before wrapping her arms around me.

"Thank you," I whisper, and she nods, her chin rubbing against my shoulder.

I grab a pair of scissors from the mess of school supplies in the first drawer I opened and hold them up against the cardstock. My fingers tremble against their rough handles. One quick finger motion, and everything Harristinks wants to promise to my mom is gone in an instant. One snip, and I might as well start packing my bags.

Success is closer than it's ever been, but now, staring at the tiny typed letters across the cardstock, I'm not sure I can bring myself to make the first cut.

"What are you doing?"

It's my second startle before six-thirty in the morning, and I'm not sure my heart can take it anymore. I jump again, shock spasming my muscles, blood pounding wildly in my head. This time, it's Mom standing in the doorway, her eyes flashing with anger.

I lower the scissors onto the desk. "I wasn't going to—"

"It looked like you were about to cut up Harrison's wedding vows," Mom says, her voice trembling the same way it did the time she caught George sneaking back into our apartment at three a.m. one weekend morning. "Are you telling me I'm wrong?"

"No, I—" My thoughts are spinning too wildly for me to catch hold of them. "I mean, that was the plan, but I just—"

"The plan?" Mom does what she's been doing best lately, and cuts me off before I can figure out how to explain the mussed-up feelings knotted together in my heart. She frowns at me, and I can see her figuring it all out. "How long has this . . . plan been going on, exactly?"

Tears are welling up behind my eyes, and I know it's too late. I have no choice but to tell her the truth. I take a deep breath, ready for the grounding of a lifetime.

"It was my idea."

I turn around to face Linnea, my lips parted in shock. Her cheeks are splotched with red, and her thin body is trembling from head to toe as Mom's eyes flick toward her.

"It's very kind of you to say that, Linnea, but I have a hard time believing it," Mom says. "You've been nothing but welcoming this entire summer, whereas, Autumn, you've been surly and dismissive and unwilling to give this place a shot from the beginning."

I stare at her. The blood is still pounding in my ears, and the anger shaking through my body matches Mom's. If we were cartoon characters, steam would be blowing out of our ears so fast, we'd fill the whole house with our anger in two seconds flat.

"You're the one who's ready to get rid of me," I shout at her. "I guess I should've known my plan wouldn't work, seeing as you love Harrison more than you love me."

Mom stares at me. "Get rid of . . . What are you talking about?"

"I heard Harrison talking to you on the phone yesterday," I say, breathing heavily, as if I've been running all morning. It feels like I've been running all summer, but clearly I wasn't fast enough. "He said he wanted to get rid of me, and you seemed perfectly fine with that idea."

Mom frowns, and I can see a million thoughts twirling behind her eyes. She's probably trying to figure out how to keep yelling at me even though I've clearly got her.

But then she blinks, and her eyes clear. "Autumn, we were talking about how sad he was about his telescope. He tried to fix it, and it's too broken. He has to get rid of the telescope. Not you. *Obviously*. No one is getting rid of you."

"But . . . but . . . but he said get rid of *her*," I sputter.

Mom closes her eyes and takes a deep breath. "He calls the telescope *her* like it's a person, Autumn. Haven't you noticed that?"

I want to tell her that Harrison has so many bizarre qualities, she can hardly expect me to keep track of every single weird thing he does, but I don't think that would help the situation, so I settle for rolling my eyes.

"Now tell me more about this ridiculous plan of yours," Mom says, crossing her arms.

"I tried to sabotage the wedding," I tell her, too mad to stop myself, too furious to care that I'm giving up on the whole plan. So *maybe* I was wrong about Harristinks wanting to get rid of me, but that doesn't change anything about the rest of the summer. It definitely doesn't change how I feel about this wedding. "You wouldn't listen to me about anything, and I didn't know what else I could do, so I got the venues to back out and I messed up the moving plans and . . . and . . ."

My brain is spinning too furiously, and I can't finish telling her all the things I did—how desperately I tried.

I just stand there, breathing hard, as if I've just run as fast as I can to the beach and back.

"And you thought that would end our relationship? What, that we would decide to just give up on the wedding because one venue canceled on us and a moving truck went astray?" Mom pinches the bridge of her nose, heaving a big sigh, and as she lowers her hand to glare at me, I feel ridiculous. She's right. My plan felt big and important because it was all I had, but the whole time it was just stupid. Doomed to fail from the beginning.

"Go to your room," Mom says. "Both of you. I have to talk to Harrison, but assume that you are grounded for a very, very long time. You can forget about visiting your friends in the city this summer after the wedding or tennis camp or doing anything but accompanying me to errands and back. I'm . . . I don't have words right now, Autumn. I really don't."

I stare at her. So that's it? Without a chance to explain, I'm banished to my room, where she doesn't have to deal with me. No matter what she said before, that sounds like she's trying to get rid of me just the same.

I don't bother to argue. I just stomp out of the room and down the hall.

Linnea pads after me.

"Autumn?" she asks, her voice quiet. "Autumn, are you—"

"No," I say shortly. I know she tried to take the fall for me, but I'm too upset to thank her.

Instead, I throw myself into bed and fold the blankets over me like I'm the world's maddest burrito. I'm exhausted from my night of not sleeping, but even though I lie there for hours, I can't manage to fall asleep.

CHAPTER SEVENTEEN

There's a knock at the door, and I know it's George before he opens it. He has such a gentle knock. I don't answer, but he opens the door anyway, and a moment later the mattress shifts as he sits next to me.

"You know, I'm really good at sabotage," he says, his voice soft as it breaks the silence.

I flip the duvet off my face to stare at him. "Now you tell me this?"

"Hey, you're the one who didn't invite me into your little plan, Raisin Bran," he says, throwing his hands up.

I scrunch my nose at him. "That rhymed."

He takes an elaborate bow, and I give him a

begrudging round of applause for his accidental rhyming skills.

"Seriously, though," he says, his expression shifting to seriousness. "Where did that come from?"

I stare at him for a moment, my stomach tightening as I examine his face. But there's only worry in his eyes, none of the fiery anger I saw all over Mom's face this morning. Breathing a sigh of relief, I flip the duvet back over my face.

George laughs, reaching over to shake my shoulder. "C'mon, Pops. It's me."

I sniffle under the blankets. George and I used to be able to talk about anything. But this summer, it's felt like he's already gone off to college. And now, with the dust fallen and the wedding almost here in spite of my best efforts, I'm embarrassed to tell him all the things I did.

"I . . ." I clear my throat, poking my nose over the duvet. "I tried to break up Mom and Harristinks."

That gets a laugh out of George. "Harristinks? Not your best nickname work, but it's a pretty good one."

"Thanks."

"Though I'm not sure he deserves it," George says fairly.

I push myself up on the mattress, resting my head against the headboard, and bite my lip. In the just over a month we've been here, Harrison has made me elaborate breakfasts, driven me anywhere I want to go, taught me to make a star map, and even made a few jokes that I struggled not to laugh at.

"I guess not," I say glumly.

George flips the duvet off me, and I screech as the chilly air hits my legs.

"We're going to the library," he says.

I stare at him. "What?"

George fixes me with a look. The ultimate you've-been-a-total-Raisin-Bran look. "We have speeches to write."

I swing my legs off the bed. I might be in the mood to lie around in bed all day, but he's right. It's the perfect way to make things right.

●●●

An hour into our work time in the library's un-air-conditioned computer room, I'm sweating from the beating summer heat, my hair is a frumpled mess, and I've had no good ideas for a speech. I can't think of anything good enough to make up for everything I've done. Mom is still furious. George had to beg her to let me leave the house with him in the first place.

This speech has to be good enough that she actually

listens to me. I need her to understand how sorry I feel, along with all the other feelings bubbling in my heart.

It's a lot to put on one piece of printer paper.

"What if you open by telling people about the Harristinks nickname?" George suggests, leaning over to look at my still-blank Word document. He printed his speech out *ages* ago.

I give him a look. "Seriously? Who's being a Raisin Bran now?"

"Maybe they'll be ready to laugh about it by then," George says, throwing his hands up.

"I tried to sabotage her wedding," I remind him. "Her whole relationship. I think it's gonna take a little more time than five days."

"At least you admit it," he says, ruffling my hair.

I turn back to my computer, chewing on my nails as I stare at the blinking cursor. What can I possibly say to make up for everything I've done?

"Mom just wants you to be part of the family, Autumn," George says.

I look up at him. We only use real names when we're really serious.

"I know," I say in a small voice.

And I do. Even though Mom hasn't done the greatest job listening this summer, she hasn't stopped talking about how much she wants us all to be a family.

It's enough that I start typing, my fingers loud against the ancient keyboard. I don't stop until I'm done, all the words coming out in one pour, until I'm ready to hit print.

I rush to the printer and snatch up the page before George can read it, holding the ink side against my T-shirt. I follow him out of the library, all my fingers crossed that Mom will like what I have to say, that she'll understand it means I'm rooting for her love. Even if I stay grounded until the end of the school year.

All I can do is hope it's enough to make her listen.

CHAPTER
EIGHTEEN

I'm on day three of my eternal grounding, but it feels like it's been eighty billion years. I'm still too nervous to show anyone the speech I wrote. I'm afraid Mom won't understand it, or that she will, but it still won't be enough.

So the printed paper is still hidden away in the dresser by my bed. I'm lying on top of said bed when Mom swings open the door to the bedroom.

"You still need a dress for the wedding," she says. Her voice is soft, but she won't meet my eye as she says it.

That's how it's been since she grounded me. A quiet tension roped between us, full of the things I'm too scared to say. Instead, I get out of bed and into jeans, hurry through an uncomfortably quiet breakfast, and follow Mom to the car.

The drive is as uncomfortably silent as breakfast—as all our meals have been since the vows incident. The radio blares between us, and each commercial break only seems to make the silence between us louder.

We drive for twenty minutes, silent on the highway, until Mom pulls into another small town that looks a lot like East Hammond. As soon as the comparison occurs to me, an odd surge of protectiveness rises in my chest. This town is nothing like East Hammond, I realize as I examine the streets we drive down. I bet it doesn't have a summer fair, or its own little beach, or a middle school student body president as cool as Linnea.

The thought surprises me. I never thought I'd want to defend East Hammond from anything. I guess the town has grown on me.

Mom parks on a little street, and we walk quietly up to a boutique with girls' party dresses displayed on mannequins in the store window.

"I thought it'd be nice for you and Linnea to both wear the same color, and George can match it with his tie," Mom says, her first words spoken aloud since we left the house. She picks a muted blue dress off the rack and shows it to me.

I nod, not trusting my voice, and take the dress from her. If there weren't this strained silence between us, I'd tell her that I love the lacy collar and that it's my favorite shade of blue. I'd tell her I love the idea of matching with Linnea.

Instead, I take the dress to the fitting rooms, where I change as fast as I can. I stare at myself in the mirror as I do the buttons that line the front of the dress. In two days, I'll be wearing this dress to match Linnea at my mom's wedding. Our parents' wedding.

A month ago, the idea made me want to run screaming for the nearest train station. Then again, a month ago, an outing with me and my mom—just the two of us—would've been my favorite afternoon.

Now I'm staring at myself in the mirror of this boutique, dreading stepping out of the fitting room because it'll mean facing Mom again.

I force myself to take a deep breath in, sapping as much strength as I can from my reflection, where I look almost grown up, ready in this fancy fabric to attend my first ever wedding. And then I pull back the thick white curtain and poke my head into the hallway.

Mom, who was slouching over her phone, stands straighter when she sees me. "Let me see the dress."

I shuffle forward, the skirt swishing around my knees. Mom's stony expression drops into a smile as she takes in the way the dress looks on me, and a wisp of hope blooms in my chest.

"Do you like it?" she asks.

I nod. "Linnea's will match?"

"Yes," Mom says, turning back to her phone. "She can pick the dress, but I'll make sure you have the same colors on."

I smile, and duck back into the changing room to put my jeans back on while Mom finds the cashier.

● ● ●

It started raining at some point when we were in the store. As we run down the street to where Mom parked the car, the light summer rain thickly coats my hair. I pull the door open and leap into the front seat. My hair drips onto my T-shirt as I watch the droplets splash against the window.

Mom clicks on her turn signal and steers us onto the highway. The red brake lights of the cars in front of us seem to stretch on forever, a gridlock of unmoving traffic trapping us in the drizzle.

She sighs when she sees it, tapping her fingers against the wheel. After a moment of sitting at a standstill, she glances at me.

"The wedding is soon," she says softly. "Are you . . .

Can you promise me that you'll be on your best behavior during the ceremony?"

I nod, not daring to make eye contact with her, and she sighs.

"I just don't understand what got ahold of you this summer," she says, leaning forward to peer through the drops on the windshield at the traffic in front of us. "How you could do this to me."

Anger flashes through me, hot against my skin. "Not everything is about you."

Mom's knuckles turn white against the steering wheel. "Watch your tone. You're already in serious trouble."

"It's true," I say, turning in my seat to face her, straining against the seat belt strapping my chest down. "Ever since we've moved, it's been all about your wedding and your new family and your new life, and I don't want any part of it."

"Autumn." Mom's voice hits that low danger-zone tone. "That is not an appropriate way to talk to me or voice your feelings."

I exhale as loudly as I can, staring out at the rows and rows of brake lights. Their red lights blur through the drizzle-coated windshield. It feels like there is no appropriate way to voice these feelings. How could there be an *appropriate* way to tell your mom you're mad at her?

"Sorry," I huff in a tone that makes it clear I'm not very *sorry* at all. "But I didn't want to move to East Hammond in the first place. Saskia and I had plans, you know. And then you and Harrison just decide that it's time for me to leave my home forever, and no one bothered to check with me on any of that. It affects me too. Not that you would know. You only want to hang out with Harrison and Linnea, ever since you started dating."

I take a deep breath. I don't think I've ever wedged so many words into just a few seconds.

The red brake light vanishes from the car in front of us for a second as we roll a few feet forward. The rain dribbles a little faster, and Mom switches on the windshield wipers. I don't dare to look in her direction. If I was reaching the danger zone earlier, I can't imagine how mad she is now. I curl my knees closer to my chest, and stare at one raindrop on the lower triangle of the windshield that the wipers can't reach. It grows fatter as the smaller drops above it trickle downward into it.

"I didn't realize you felt that way," Mom says quietly, finally breaking the silence.

I dare a peek at her from the corner of my eye, and it almost looks like she's on the verge of tears. It makes a hard lump clog up my throat. I haven't seen Mom cry in, like, two years.

Since she started dating Harrison, I realize.

Swallowing, I flick my eyes back to the windshield. Another droplet falls into my fat raindrop. It's one too many—the drop trembles against the glass once before sliding down the windshield.

"I thought this would be good for our family," she says quietly.

"It's just good for you," I say. The car jerks forward again as the traffic eases for a moment before the rows of brake lights snap back on.

"It is good for me," Mom says after a moment. "Is that so hard to accept? That after everything that's happened, something might finally, finally be good for me?"

"But it's *so bad* for me, and you don't even care." I tug on the end of my braid as I talk. The faintest hint of red that always comes out in summer has weaved its way into my brown hair, glinting with rainwater.

Mom closes her eyes. Her whole face sags, like my words have hooked into her pores to tug her skin down. "I didn't know it was so bad for you."

"You never asked," I mutter.

"I'm trying, Autumn. I got you the tennis camp so you could get settled, make friends. You have to try too. It's a change for all of us. You have to give it a shot."

"None of that is what I want." My lower lip trembles.

"What is it that you want, then?" She's finally asking the question I've been waiting for, but her tone is exasperated, mad, like she's annoyed she has to ask it.

I hunch against the car door, staring out at the traffic. It feels like we've barely moved. Mom hasn't listened to me about anything, ever since she started calling Harrison her boyfriend. How am I supposed to talk to her about what I want now? Especially now, with this. Even if I understand my feelings a little better, I still don't know what the right words are.

"I want my home. I want my family back the way it used to be, when I knew right where I fit in with just the three of us. I . . . I want Saskia," I tell her.

Mom huffs. "It's normal to miss your friends, Autumn, but you'll make new ones."

Friend. I press my tongue against my teeth, turning the word over in my mind. It's not the right one. I don't know what the right word is, but I know *friend* is the wrong one.

"I don't miss her like a friend."

Mom's eyebrows knit together. I stare out the window, shriveling into my seat. We round a bend in the road, and if I crane my neck, I can see an accident up ahead. Two men in bright yellow vests direct the cars around a semicircle of orange cones jutting out into our lane.

"What do you mean, you don't miss her like a friend?" Mom says.

"Just that," I say. I force myself to straighten my posture and stretch out my legs in front of me. I don't need to shrink away. "She's not like my other friends."

Mom smiles, and I can tell from the condescending gentleness of her features that she still doesn't get it. "It's nice to have such a close friend. You and Saskia can keep in—"

"I have a crush on her," I blurt, before she can say anything else about *keeping in touch* or *friendship* or anything else that so completely misses the point.

Mom's lips part and her eyebrows flash upward for just a moment. She blinks, closing her mouth, and she almost succeeds in hiding the effort it takes to bring her face back to normal.

"A crush?" Mom looks over at me.

"Yes," I say softly. "And Saskia? She's . . . she's a girl, Mom. As in, not a boy, not like everyone else has a crush on. As in, a girl like Dana has."

"Dana?"

I sigh. Mom's focusing on all the wrong things in this story. "The counselor from the tennis camp you made me go to. I saw her holding hands with a girl. Same as me and Saskia. She says if I like a girl, I shouldn't let her go."

"You're only twelve. You'll have lots of crushes—" Mom says.

"Not. The. Point." I square my shoulders. "None of that is the point."

We roll forward a little more. We're almost at the accident. I can see the front hood of the car, crumpled like a piece of paper left at the bottom of a backpack.

"What is the point, then?" Mom asks as she hits the brakes. The car stops a little too fast, and my body jerks forward against the seat belt.

"The *point* is that we moved away from our house and then I thought I might have a crush on my best friend and I had all these questions, and I wanted to talk to you about them, but you only want to tell me about making friends with Linnea and settling into stupid East Hammond and wedding cake flavors that all taste like Play-Doh anyway. And you never want to hang out with me anymore. We used to go on picnics and make up board games, and now all you have time for is making Linnea your new daughter and forcing me to do tennis camp so you don't have to see me around anymore. It was supposed to be just you and me after George goes to college, and now there's no room for me at all."

I feel like I should be crying, spreading everything that I've kept bottled up inside out into the space between us like this, but I guess I used up all my tears this summer, because my eyes stay dry. My throat doesn't clog up. My fingers shake a little. I tuck them under my thighs.

Mom doesn't say anything for a long time. She stares at the accident. We're almost right up to it now. There's only a few cars between us and the man in the yellow traffic vest.

I fidget against my seat, peeking at her face out of the corner of my eye. I can't make out her expression at all. It's too perfectly neutral, and I wonder if she's doing it on purpose, working hard again to hide her feelings from me. It makes my heart beat double fast. What if she tells me I'm too young to understand how a crush feels, that I'll change my mind about Saskia? What if she tells me none of it matters? That I'll make new friends and learn to have a crush on a boy?

She stays quiet, still, as we roll right up next to the dented car. Then she reaches across the gear stick between us to squeeze my hand. "I'm so sorry, Autumn."

I blink, swallowing. I don't know what I expected her response to be, but it wasn't that.

"I had no idea you had so much going on. I thought you were just unwilling to give East Hammond a fair shot. I want you to love it there, because I love it there, and I love Harrison. It's been a long time since I've been in love," she adds, giving me a little smile. "After your dad and I got divorced, I never thought that would happen for me again. I was so happy when it did. I guess I lost sight of how it affected you. And I'm so sorry, Autumn, because you and George are the most important parts of my life."

I must have a few tears left over after all, because my cheeks are wet. With my free hand, I wipe them dry.

"I didn't mean to make you feel like I don't have time for you anymore," Mom says quietly. "I was trying to give you space to get to know our new family members, and our new home. But just because our family's growing doesn't mean there's less room for you in my heart. I want you to know that. Do you want to invite Saskia to the wedding?"

The traffic officer waves at Mom. We roll past the accident, and, just like that, we leave the traffic behind. The cars loosen, and Mom speeds up. We zip past the waterlogged trees lining the highway.

"Really?"

"She's important to you," Mom says. "Of course I want her there."

My thoughts tumble together. Every inch of me is dying to see Saskia again.

But what if she doesn't want to come? She's been busy with Delilah all summer. What if she somehow figured out how I feel about her, and doesn't even want to be my friend anymore?

"Can I think about it?"

"Sure, honey," Mom says. She glances at me out of the corner of her eye. "I'm sorry I wasn't around for you to talk to about everything you've been dealing with."

"It's okay," I say. Mom tuts, and I roll my eyes. "I accept your apology. I'm sorry I was"—I pause, trying to remember her wording—"unwilling to give East Hammond a shot."

Mom gives me a small smile. "I don't think I'm the person you have to apologize to for that."

My forehead wrinkles as I remember Linnea's Welcome Home poster and her hopeful smile when she waved me into her house. The way I refused to join in when she and her friends tried to ask me questions. How I pretended to hate the summer fair even though it was objectively really cool. The broken telescope, already swept away.

"You're right," I say. "Can we make a stop in town on the way home?"

Mom nods, clicking her turn signal on as she shifts to an exit lane. I smile in spite of myself. I can still make this right.

CHAPTER
NINETEEN

"Where do you want to go?" Mom asks as we roll off the highway. She turns right into town instead of speeding past it to go straight home.

I twist my lips, trying to remember what Linnea said when she told me about how much she wants a sister. "We need snacks, and face masks, and nail polish, and maybe some makeup? Oh, and a card. Definitely a card."

Mom laughs, pulling over in front of the CVS. "What are you planning?"

I pop my door open and spring out of the car without answering her question. It's stopped pouring, but the smell of fresh rain hangs heavy in the air, like it's still drying off.

I skip across the parking lot to the CVS, as fast as I can get there. Even though it's nighttime and pretty cool out, the AC blasts in the doorway. I shiver as soon as I walk through the door. I run up and down the aisles, scooping up all the materials I need from the shelf. Mom walks after me, a box of garbage bags in her hands and a bewildered expression on her face.

"What do you need all that for?" she asks, eyeing all the stuff in my hands as I lead her to the cash register.

"I need to apologize to Linnea," I tell her, getting in line behind a young woman with strawberry-blond hair and a man in a baseball tee buying what looks like enough Phish Food ice cream to sustain a small country.

If Linnea and I are going to be proper sisters, the kind who share secrets as easily as they do clothes, then I have to do more than say I'm sorry to make up for how much I've pushed her away. I have to show her I mean it. Like Harrison said, I have to make it right.

I grab a couple packs of M&M's and add them on top of the purple nail polish I picked out when we get to the cash register. Mom purses her lips, but she must still feel bad, because she doesn't say anything about processed sugar as she pays.

When we're back in the car, I balance the card I picked out over my knees and write as carefully as I can as Mom drives us home. The car dips into a few potholes on the way, sending my hand jerking across the page, so the end result is still scrawlier than I would have liked.

Dear Linnea,

I'm sorry for everything. Can we be sisters?

Love, Autumn

It's simple, but I hope she can see the feeling behind every word.

Mom pulls up in front of Harrison's house—our house—and the nervous butterflies in my stomach kick into high gear. My gut churns as I push the car door open, crossing my fingers hard together. I hope this is enough. I hope she knows how sorry I am, even if she doesn't forgive me right away.

I follow Mom into the house, the handles of the CVS bag bunched up in my hand.

Part of me wants to run down the hall to our bedroom, show Linnea what I got, get it all over with and skip to the fun part. Instead, I walk slowly, trailing my feet against the carpet, giving myself more time to be afraid.

The bedroom door is closed, but I can see the light shining through the crack between the door and the carpet. I knock gently.

"Come in," she calls.

When I open the door, I see her sitting up in her bed. Her knees are up, the blanket bunching around her waist.

"Hey," I say. "I want to say I'm sorry. For everything I've done this summer."

"It's fine," Linnea says with a shrug. "You've made it pretty clear you don't want to be part of this family."

I shuffle over to her bed, swallowing. "I know I've been saying that, but I was wrong," I say, laying the bag next to her. "I'm really excited about it, because it means I get to have you as a sister."

Linnea looks down into the bag, and the corners of her lips twitch as she fights a smile.

"I thought you weren't into it," she says quietly.

"I wasn't," I say. "I was wrong. I'm really sorry."

I slide the card across the mattress. "Want to have a sister slumber party tonight?"

Linnea can't fight her smile anymore, but she ducks her head, not saying anything.

"Our first of many, so I went all out. Nail polish, face masks, enough candy for us to get super, super, *super* sick."

I cross my fingers under the handles of the plastic bag. I want her to see that this is more than just a bag of stuff I picked out at CVS. This is my way of offering her what she wanted: time shared together, just the two of us, as sisters.

Linnea laughs, and finally kicks her blanket off.

"Fine, but only because you got candy," she says, but her smile is huge.

"Meet you back in our room after dinner?" I say, as if we don't do that every night.

Linnea's face lights up, and it's answer enough for me.

Dinner passes at a snail's pace. I only eat a little, saving room for the full stash of M&M's that I spent the afternoon daydreaming about. Slower still is the movie night we have after. I barely register a single scene of the movie George picks. My ears are buzzing too loudly with excitement. As soon as it ends, Linnea and I say our good nights and dash back to our room.

I pull the bag of stuff next to me as I drop to the floor. "Should we start with the face masks?"

I fish through the bag until I find the pink-wrapped

face mask buried under the nail polish. "I've never actually done one of these before."

"Me neither." Linnea giggles as she peels hers open. A thin sheer plastic-looking mask dangles from her fingertips. "Do I just . . . stick this on my face?"

I scan the instructions. "Looks like it. I think you gotta line this bit up with your nose."

I help her pat the slippery mask down against her skin. When I pull my hands away, I burst out laughing.

Linnea's face reddens under the mask. "What? Did I do it wrong?"

"No," I say, coughing down my laugh. "You just look like . . ."

I don't know how to describe it. Her face looks a bit like a weird scary robot with a flat nose and creepy eye slits. "C'mon."

I pull the door open, and we tiptoe to the bathroom, careful not to alert anyone else to the fact that we're still awake. I'm not ready for Mom to make us end the sleepover and go to bed just yet.

When we get to the bathroom, I flip the lights on, and it's Linnea's turn to double over with laughter when she sees her face in the mirror.

"Oh, we gotta get one of these on you," she says, pulling me back to the bedroom. I run after her, laughing.

After we wash the masks off—my skin is seriously

soft, it's almost worth looking like a robo-snake—we do each other's nails. She does an awful job with mine, and my whole fingertips end up covered in purple goop. It's nothing at all like when Saskia does it, her brush curving artfully around the edges of my nails as if my fingertips are one of her canvases, but that doesn't mean it's bad. This can be its own thing.

Well, objectively, the manicure is pretty bad. But my sides still hurt from laughing.

"Let me show you how it's done," I say, taking her hand into my lap.

Turns out, I spoke too soon. Between all the giggling and a brief skirmish for the blue M&M's, Linnea's fingertips end up an even bigger mess than mine.

"So," Linnea says, wiggling her fingers in the air to dry out her freshly clompy purple nails. "Who do you like?"

She puts on a silly voice, like she's one of the popular girls at a sleepover in an old movie. It makes me laugh.

"Actually, I like . . ." I pause, chewing on the inside of my cheek. Should I tell her?

I take a deep breath. Sisters, right? Secrets are like clothes here. Swappable.

"I like this girl from my . . . my old school. Saskia."

Linnea grins. "That's so cool. Did you know Dana

has a girlfriend? Laurie. She's the lifeguard at the public pool."

I exhale, and it feels like it's the first time I've gotten to do that all summer. All my muscles unwind with the breath. "I saw them holding hands at camp."

"Does she like you back?" Linnea asks. "Saskia?"

"I don't know," I admit.

"Tell me about her," Linnea says.

And I do. I tell her about our adventures in the city, and how I spent all summer trying to get in touch with her, and how I don't really know what to say, but it doesn't matter because she only answers my texts half the time anyway these days.

"I had no idea," she says when I finish telling her about Delilah. "I can't believe she did that to you."

"I don't know what to do," I say. "It was just tough because I wanted to talk to my mom about it, but she's been all wrapped up in wedding planning. Which is why I was being such a brat about it."

Linnea nudges her toe with mine. "It's okay. You could've talked to me."

I smile into my knees. "I will next time."

"You should invite her to the wedding," Linnea says, and she sounds so sure of it that I find myself nodding.

"Maybe you're right," I say. Saskia might say no,

but it's the only way to get answers. "I'll tell Mom to call her mom in the morning."

"I don't want to tell Katie and Erica who I like because I tried to tell him and he laughed at me," Linnea says suddenly, the words coming out of her mouth so fast that I have trouble understanding her.

I blink, processing what she's said. "He what?"

"I told him I liked him at summer camp last year and he laughed and said he didn't like me back," she whispers. "I thought he liked me too. I thought we were having a moment. Turns out, I was super wrong. I didn't want to tell them because it's embarrassing."

"He sounds awful," I tell her. "Besides, aren't there, like, a zillion people at your school? You'll find someone better. And it's not embarrassing to try."

She wraps her arms around my shoulder, pulling me down into a hug. My head lands on her shoulder, and I hug her waist. In all the time I spent stressing about the attention I'd lose when my family got bigger, I never thought about everything I stood to gain. Now, hugging Linnea, whose face smells like pomegranate from the face mask and whose fingers are staining my pajama seams purple, I feel like maybe Mom's whole wedding idea isn't so bad after all.

"I told them I don't want to talk about it, though," Linnea tells me when we pull apart. "Like you said.

And you were right—they weren't mad. They agreed not to bring it up anymore."

"I always am," I say, tossing my hair, and Linnea giggles.

"I made you something," she says. "Want to see?"

I nod eagerly, and she gets up to grab something from the desk. When she plops back down next to me, I see it's the map I drew, the one where I crossed out all the places where she sabotaged my escape plan.

"I'm sorry I lied to you," she says, pushing the paper toward me. It's covered in new labels and the drawings are colored in. "I used it to plan some new places I want to show you."

I can't stop staring at it. There are so many places she's marked. Some, like the beach, I already know, but most are a total mystery, and I realize I can't wait to find out what they are. I can't wait to *get to know* East Hammond after all.

"I'm the one who's sorry," I say. "I shouldn't have been trying to break up the wedding in the first place."

"The sabotage was kind of fun, though," Linnea says with a laugh.

I shake my head at her. "I can't believe your plan worked."

I stifle a yawn as I straighten, but Linnea sees it.

"Maybe we should go to bed," she says. "The big

day is almost here. And the rehearsal dinner is tomorrow."

"What's the point of a rehearsal dinner anyway?" I ask as I climb into bed. "Like, do we really need to practice eating?"

Linnea giggles. "You gotta use your fanciest table manners."

"Drink water with my pinkie out?"

"And the adults have to smell the wine for a thousand years before they take a sip."

She switches off the light and jumps under her covers. I wriggle lower onto my pillow so that my chin is tucked under the blanket.

"I'm going to make sure Saskia comes to the wedding," I say into the dark.

"I can't wait to meet her," Linnea whispers back. There's a stretch of silence, and then she clears her throat. "Thank you. This was perfect."

"It's what sisters are for," I whisper back.

I smile as I snuggle into the blankets. I should sleep, but my chest is too buoyant—lighthearted and carefree—to settle down. I want Saskia to meet Linnea too. I want to tell her all the things I'm feeling, tell her how my summer's been, hear about hers.

But first I have to invite her to the wedding.

CHAPTER
TWENTY

I'm buzzing.

My skin is a live wire. It's a miracle the hairdresser and the makeup artist manage to touch me without catching on fire from the electricity crackling off me.

As soon as the artist is done adding mascara to my look—which Mom insisted had to be as natural as possible—I spin around in my getting-ready chair.

"Did she call yet?" I ask for the fifth time since we got up this morning.

Mom, who's sitting in her own getting-ready chair, gives me a look. "Autumn. Who waited until after the rehearsal dinner to ask me to call Saskia's mom and invite them to the wedding?"

"Me," I admit.

In my defense, my plan had been to call Saskia myself. The morning after my sister slumber party with Linnea, I plucked up the courage to dial her. She didn't answer.

Instead, she sent me a text back over an hour later.

> **Saskia:** Sorry! I'm at camp for the day. What's up?

I hadn't gotten the courage to call her again. What if she never answers me? I tried to text her instead, but the entire day, I fretted about what would happen if she never texted me back. I was so busy worrying, I barely noticed the time go by until suddenly, there I was at the rehearsal dinner, and it was too late. So I begged Mom to call her mom as soon as we got home.

Voice mail.

Mom left a voice mail, and we still haven't heard back.

She must see the panic in my eyes now, because she reaches around the hairdresser to squeeze my hand. "If they don't get it in time, we'll find another day for you to see each other, okay?"

I nod, but the thought of Saskia not being at my mom's wedding makes me want to cry, threatening the mascara that the makeup artist so carefully applied to my face.

Linnea, who looks amazing with her blond hair lightly curled, gives me a hug.

"I'm sure she'll come," she whispers.

I give her a small smile back, but my stomach is too knotted up to say anything in response.

Mom turns back to the mirror, watching as the hairdresser puts the finishing touches on her look. She's wearing her auburn hair down, with white flowers braided into one side. The part of me that planned to stop this wedding hates to admit it, but she looks beautiful.

As soon as the hairdresser is done, Mom stands slowly. Her hair rustles around her shoulders, her dress falling to the floor as she rises. Linnea and I squeeze hands as we take her in. She looks like a bride.

Looking at her, I feel the opposite of how I thought I would. Instead of prickling with the failure of my plan, I'm sort of in awe. Mom is all glowing and smiley, in a way I haven't seen her look in a long time.

Something might finally, finally be good for me. That's what she said to me in the car as we were driving back from dress shopping. And now here she is, on her wedding morning, looking like she might burst from feeling so happy. Seeing her like that makes me happy too.

Without thinking, I cross the multipurpose room at the venue we're using to get ready for the wedding and wrap my arms around her.

Behind me, I can hear the photographer's camera going nuts as she documents this, my blue dress crushed against Mom's bridal gown as she hugs me back so tight, I can barely breathe.

"You look beautiful," I whisper, and Mom kisses the top of my head.

"So do you," she whispers back.

I pull away from her, smiling. I just wish Saskia were here to share this moment with me. I've never been through a major life moment without Saskia by my side, and I never thought I'd go to something as huge as my mom's wedding without her.

"She'll come if she gets the voice mail in time, honey," Mom says, seeing me open my mouth to ask yet again.

But guests are already starting to arrive. Mom sends Linnea and me to the front hall so we can direct guests to the event room where the wedding will be taking place. The guests fill the rows of folding chairs lining the space, their voices echoing across the room. Every time a new set of footsteps precedes someone rounding the corner, I perk up, my shoulders slumping forward again when anyone but Saskia appears at the doors.

By the time Linnea and I have to take our seats in the front row, Saskia still hasn't shown up. I can't even ask Mom if she's heard from Mrs. Stone, either, because she's waiting in the back to make her big entrance. I take my seat next to Linnea, trying not to look too glum.

"If she doesn't get the message, I'm sure she'll want to see you another time," Linnea says. "Sometime soon."

"I hope so," I say, twisting my fingers together in my lap. "I just want to talk to her."

"You'll get to," Linnea says, and her voice sounds so sure that for a moment it makes me feel better.

The crowd around us quiets as the officiant, a friend of Harrison's who introduced him to Mom at a party, welcomes everyone to the wedding. Mom decided she didn't want any bridesmaids, so as soon as the music starts, she walks down the aisle, her arm looped through George's elbow.

They stop at the end of the aisle, and Mom shoots me a wink as George hugs her before she joins Harrison by the officiant at the front of the room. The wink warms my heart, as good as a hug, a perfect reminder that, even though our family is growing right in front of me, there's still room for me. The ceremony starts, and I find myself blinking fast to hide the tears blurring my vision. I can't let myself happy cry at my mom's wedding in front of all these people. That's just embarrassing.

The officiant says, "You may now kiss the bride," and I wish he hadn't, because it means Harrison leans over and kisses Mom. Ew.

Still, Linnea and I exchange smiles, and I reach over to squeeze her hand.

"I now pronounce you husband and wife," the officiant says, and the room erupts into cheers.

I can't help but smile as tears well up in my eyes. Just like that, Harrison is my stepdad. Linnea is officially my sister. My family has almost doubled in size in the span of one quick ceremony.

And Saskia isn't here to see it.

• • •

We have the reception in the library's garden. Mom spent all of last night with her fingers tightly crossed for good weather, and the universe clearly heard her wish. The sky is endless blue, the occasional rolling white cloud shading the tables propped up on the lawn.

We take our seats at the tables set up along the grass. Katie and Erica are at the table next to ours, and they wave brightly. I return their waves cheerily. Harrison (and it *kills* me to admit this) was right: it'll be nice to have friends on the first day of school. And it helps to know that they took it well when Linnea set her boundary with them about crush talk.

The evening starts with champagne (or, in my case, apple juice in a fancy glass) and speeches. Mom's best friend goes first, giving a teary speech about how happy she is that Mom's found happiness. Harrison's best man goes next, and none of his jokes are funny. I'd expect nothing less from anyone Harrison calls a friend.

George goes before me, and his speech is so good that it gets me worried about what I've planned to say.

"I just can't believe you waited until I'm out of here before bringing this amazing guy into our family," he finishes, and gets yet another huge laugh from the group before everyone takes another sip of their drink.

George passes the microphone to me, and my hands are so clammy that I'm worried I'll drop it. I grip it extra hard between my fingers, taking a deep breath to steady my shaky nerves. And exhale straight into the microphone, sending a loud breathy huff through the outdoor space.

Nice one, Autumn. Off to a great start.

"Sorry," I say when I see George cringe. He rolls his

eyes at me, motioning with a twirl of his finger for me to get going, but he's grinning. He'll be making fun of me for this for years to come, I bet.

"I, uh, well." There are *so many* people looking at me. I lift my printer paper a bit higher so I can hide behind the speech as I read. "I wasn't always the biggest fan of this wedding. In fact, I did sort of a lot to stop it from happening."

There are a few titters from the crowd, and I can feel Mom's eyes glaring into the side of my face.

"I completely disorganized the moving-in process, and if you know my mom, you know that's basically the same as failing all my classes and running away to join the circus on the same day."

That gets a laugh out of her best friends, and I breathe a sigh of relief.

"I also ruined their date nights and Harrison's cooking," I add, which gets Harrison to chuckle as he realizes that I sugared his tomato sauce on purpose. "I got all the wedding venues to back out of hosting the wedding. And I threw up at the cake tasting. Not," I say as the crowd giggles, "on purpose, but when you're on a sabotage mission, you take what you can get."

I shift my weight as a light breeze kicks up around us. "But even though every part of my plan was obviously genius, none of it worked. I mean, look at this

wedding. It's beautiful." I'm met with appreciative applause, so I pause for a minute before I go on. "I realized
Mom and Harrison love each other so much, nothing
I do could break them up. And now that I see how
happy my mom is with Harrison, I'm so sorry I ever
tried to. I'm so happy I get to be part of this family."

"Yeah, yeah, rub it in," George calls from his seat.

"Shut up, Cocoa Puffs," I say, accidentally into the
microphone, and blush as Linnea giggles at me. "Anyway. I love my new family a lot, and I can't believe I
ever wanted out of it. I can't imagine being anywhere
else anymore."

Mom gets up and pulls me into the tightest hug I've
ever been in. I squeeze her back, careful not to muss
the lace of her dress.

"I love you so much," she whispers.

"I love you too."

She lets me go, and just like that, the speeches are
over and it's time for dinner.

I'm at a table with Linnea and George. Mom and
Harrison—who I guess I should start calling H-Dad,
even though it really doesn't work as well as S-Mom—
are supposed to be at the table with us, but they got up
as soon as the speeches ended to greet all the guests
and haven't had time to come back. Every time they
take a step forward, they're immediately surrounded

by a new group of guests eager to congratulate them, take pictures, and catch up.

George grins as yet another friend of Mom's rushes up to pull her into a hug. "Looks like the sibling squad will be dining alone this afternoon."

"And it's practically our last meal before Tufts," I whine.

George ruffles my hair, and Linnea swats his hand away.

"Those curls are professional," she informs him.

"Yeah," I say, and we high-five over our plates.

George narrows his eyes at us. "Not sure I'm the world's hugest fan of the fact that my sisters out-number me now."

"Get used to it, Cocoa Puffs," I say, and Linnea giggles.

"What's up with the cereal names?" she asks.

George tells her the story of my five-year-old tantrum as I scan the crowd yet again. I've done it so many times that the hope of seeing Saskia has dulled. It feels more like picking at a scab now—I know nothing good can come of it, but I can't help myself.

This time, though, I spot a figure lingering by the back doorway of the library. A small figure I recognize all too well.

Without stopping to explain myself, I'm out of my

seat and dashing across the lawn, zipping through the crowd as fast as I can so that no one grabs me and tries to congratulate me on my recent acquisition of an H-Dad. I don't stop until I've raced up the winding cobblestone path to the doorway where Saskia is standing.

I'm breathing heavily when I reach her, winded from the shock of spotting her across the reception. She's wearing a pale pink dress, her dark hair twisted into a thick braid.

For a moment, all I can do is stare at her in disbelief. She's here. Actually here.

And then, before I can say anything at all, she pulls me into a hug.

"Hi," she whispers into my hair.

I clutch her tightly back. "You came."

"Of course." She pulls away, her eyes shining with tears, constellations pooling around her irises. "I brought you something. A wedding gift."

I laugh. "I'm not the one getting married."

"Well, I thought, after seeing your mom marry Harristinks," Saskia says.

"He's not so bad," I tell her. "Once I got to know him."

She grins as she reaches down to the plastic bag sitting in a heap by her feet, pulling out a small canvas. "This was my art piece I put up at the camp art show."

I gasp when I see it.

It's our map, where we planned our summer adventures. I can see a few of our stickers and sketched arrows and notes, but she's painted over it with a picture of the two of us, when we sat in the corner of our favorite ice cream shop and ate mint chocolate chip ice cream. Before everything else was ruined.

It's beautiful. I take it from her, my fingers trembling as I stare down at it, trying to absorb every part of the canvas.

"I'm sorry," she says.

My eyes flick to her. A deep red blush creeps across her cheeks.

"I wanted to talk to you," she says, and her voice is thick with tears. "I've just had all these"—she twists her fingers in the air in front of her chest—"feelings? Questions? All year. I wanted to talk to you, but I didn't know what to say." She blinks fast, as though trying to keep the tears in. "I still don't. So it was easier to just make new friends and ignore your calls."

I blink, shock reeling through me. I know exactly what Saskia's trying to say, even though she can't actually say it, because the same questions have been hitting me since I moved away. Since I started thinking about crushes.

But I had no idea she'd spent the whole summer feeling the same way.

"East Hammond sucked at first," I say instead. "I had to share my room with my new stepsister. Mom was so busy with wedding stuff that she didn't have any time to hang out with me, even worse than when she started dating Harrison in the first place. And everyone knows how to ride a bike." I pause, staring hard at the painting so that I don't meet her eye. "And you're not here."

"New York sucks without you too," she says quietly.

Her words make my heart beat faster, not with fear this time, but with something bubbly and good. The kind of good that makes me smile before I realize I'm smiling as I remember our last outing before Mom dropped the East Hammond bomb all over my life. I'd planned a stop on our way home from school one day, at a Beatles themed pop-up store, because even though I don't really care about music, I know they're one of Saskia's favorite bands.

Linnea's too, now that I think of it.

Saskia knew an ice cream place "close by," which ended up being a fifteen-minute walk out of our way. We got really lost, but we got to pet six dogs as we found our way back to the subway.

"East Hammond is better now," I tell her. "Harrison is actually pretty cool. And Linnea is the greatest sister ever. But I miss you." My voice drops to a whisper. "I had questions and feelings too."

She doesn't say anything, but she lifts her hand, reaching for me until her fingers press against mine. I slip my hand under hers, our fingers intertwining.

I don't say anything either. I still don't have words, but maybe the answers I've been looking for are there, in the space between our hands. The silence tucks around us like a blanket.

I've held Saskia's hand before. When I pull her across the street. When she leads me toward an unplanned part of our latest adventure.

This time, it's different. I've never held her hand because I want to hold her hand. And I think that Mom was wrong when she told me that saying "make the Yuletide gay" is old-fashioned.

I think it means happy in this context too.

I still don't have the right words, but telling her the truth has made all the panic I felt disappear, like all I had to do was reach across the space between us and take her hand. Like that's what I was supposed to do all along, and I just now figured it out.

I glance back at the reception, where guests are

getting up from their assigned tables and turning the grass into a dance floor as the band strikes up. Grinning, I turn back to Saskia.

"Want to meet my sister?"

She nods, but doesn't let go of my hand as we walk back down to my sibling squad table. Linnea's eyes flit down to our interlocked hands before she meets my gaze, and she waggles her eyebrows at me. I roll my eyes, but I'm smiling huge as I introduce them.

"It's *so* nice to meet you," Linnea tells Saskia. "I've heard so much about you. Autumn talks about you all the time."

Welp. That's just about the most embarrassing thing she could possibly have said.

"Do you guys want to dance?" I say quickly before Saskia has time to tease me about the fact that I think about her incessantly.

Linnea nods, and I lead them out to the makeshift dance floor in the middle of the lawn, and we join Katie and Erica as they jump around to the beat. I sway awkwardly between Linnea and Saskia, realizing as she twirls next to me that I've just asked my crush to dance, a decision that is even more mortifying than Linnea's teasing.

But then Saskia reaches over and takes my hand

again, and my bone-deep embarrassment eases a bit. Sure, she might be a crush now, but she's still *Saskia*. My best friend.

Here on the dance floor with me and my sister.

I look between the two of them, my smile huge as the band starts playing an upbeat song. And we start bopping to the beat, all of us screaming the lyrics at the same time until we're out of breath, dancing together under the endless sky in this once-awful wonderful place I get to call home.

ACKNOWLEDGMENTS

Autumn's story is so special to me, and it's even more special when I think about all the incredible people who helped me bring this book to life.

Penny Moore, my brilliant agent, thank you so much for seeing past the mess of my first draft and helping me turn this story into one I love so much. You're my hero always, and I can never thank you enough!

I'm eternally thankful to Kelsey Horton, my incredible editor. Thank you for always seeing exactly what my work needs. I'm in awe of everything you do!

Thank you to the whole team at Delacorte Press who worked to make this book the best it could be, especially my copyeditors, Carrie Andrews, Alison Kolani, and Colleen Fellingham, and Celia Krampien, whose brilliant cover art perfectly captures this story.

A very special thank-you to Caron Levis, thesis

advisor extraordinaire. I couldn't have written Autumn's story without you.

Infinite love and thank-yous to my coven: Annette Christie, Andrea Contos, Sonia Hartl, Susan Lee, Kelsey Rodkey, and Rachel Solomon. Thank you for the soft-ent, for the unconditional support through genuine struggles and minor inconveniences alike, and for filling my life with your love, humor, and Wordle scores.

I am blessed to work alongside so many incredible writers and friends who make my work and my life richer. Thank you, Evelyn Luchs, Marisa Kanter, Carlyn Greenwald, Courtney Kae, Karis Rogerson, and Jenny Howe. Special thanks to this story's early readers, especially Trisha Kelly, AJ Sass, and Emily Howard. Your feedback and support were invaluable.

To my much-loved riot-turned-book-club—Nadja, Victoria, Haley, Ace, Ashley, and Finn—thank you for your support and for making sure I read at least one book/experience at least one critical thought each month.

An extremely special shout-out to my stitch-and-bitch pals: Haley, Abby, Shelby, Jules, Shannon, and Amanda—with of course much love and gratitude to the lads, Jack, Jimmy, and Robert—for letting me bitch incessantly and stitch just a little bit. My life is better because you are in it.

Karen and Luke: I couldn't do any of this without you. Thank you for your endless support and your strong belief in classroom couches. Special thanks always to our classes of '21, '22, '23, and '24 for letting me write this book between reading blocks.

Thank you to my family for always supporting me, and for always reading my books (even though only one of you is actually a teen girl). Your support of my writing and of everything else means the world to me.

Many thanks to Erin for always retweeting my book news even though you have a private account, and also for marrying me. You're a star.

I owe so much to all the readers, bloggers, booksellers, teachers, and librarians who support my work. You truly mean more than I can put into words. Thank you, thank you, thank you.

ABOUT THE AUTHOR

Auriane Desombre is a middle-school teacher and freelance editor. She holds an MA in English Literature and an MFA in Creative Writing for Children and Young Adults. She lives in Los Angeles with her dog, Sammy, who is a certified bad boy. She is the author of *I Think I Love You*. *The Sister Split* is her middle-grade debut.